Singing to the Sun

and other magical tales

written by
VIVIAN FRENCH

illustrated by
CHRIS FISHER

WALKER BOOKS
AND SUBSIDIARIES

LONDON • BOSTON • SYDNEY

For Caz
with all my love
X X X

This collection first published 2001 by Walker Books Ltd
87 Vauxhall Walk, London SE11 5HJ

This edition published 2001

2 4 6 8 10 9 7 5 3 1

Text © 1993, 1995, 1998, 1999, 2001 Vivian French
Illustrations © 1993, 1995, 1999, 2001 Chris Fisher

This book has been typeset in Calligraphic 810 BT

Printed and bound in Great Britain by
The Guernsey Press Co. Ltd

British Library Cataloguing in Publication Data:
a catalogue record for this book is
available from the British Library

ISBN 0-7445-8234-2

Contents

Tomkin and the
Three-Legged Stool

There was once a little tailor called Tomkin. He
had no mother, no father, no brothers and no
sisters. He had nothing that belonged to him except
for his needles, his reels of cotton, his scissors, and
a three-legged stool, but he sang and he whistled
as he worked.

One night Tomkin had a dream. He dreamed
that instead of hard bread and water for his supper
he had hot cabbage soup with soft white rolls. He
dreamed that instead of sleeping on a cold and
draughty bench he had a warm and cosy bed with
thick red blankets. He dreamed that instead of sitting all day on a little wooden stool with three

7

legs, he sat on a golden throne.

Tomkin sat up on his bench and rubbed his eyes.

"Well!" he said. "That was a good dream – the best I've ever had. Hot cabbage soup! Thick red blankets! And me a king – whatever can it mean?" He scratched his head, and looked at his three-legged stool.

"What do you think?" he asked.

The three-legged stool turned around twice and bowed.

"I think Your Majesty should go out and find your kingdom," it said.

"You're quite right," said Tomkin. "All I do here is mend shirts and stockings and sew on the mayor's buttons twice a week. I'll be off right away." He hopped off the bench and packed a bag with all his needles, three reels of cotton and a pair of sharp scissors.

"Now I'm ready," he said, but he didn't go out through the door.

"What are you waiting for?" asked the three-legged stool.

"I was wondering if I'd be lonely, travelling all the way to my kingdom on my own," said Tomkin.

"It might be near, or it might be far," said the three-legged stool. "Shall I come with you?"

"Yes, please," said Tomkin, "and when I'm king I promise I'll make you prime minister."

The stool spun round on one leg and sang:

"Promises, promises, one, two, three,
A king will never remember me."

"Oh, yes, I will," said Tomkin, and they went through the door together.

Tomkin walked along the road with a hop, a skip and a jump, and the three-legged stool trundled along beside him. They walked through a forest and over a hill and down into the valley on the other side. Sometimes they talked, and sometimes they were silent, and sometimes Tomkin whistled a tune and the stool danced on its three wooden legs.

Down in the valley was a wide river and Tomkin and the three-legged stool came to a stop.

"Oh, dear," said Tomkin, "I can't swim! Do you think my kingdom is on this side or the other side of the river?"

"It might be far, or it might be near," said the

9

stool. "But as to swimming – just throw me in and hold on tightly!"

Tomkin waded into the rushing water, holding on to the stool. The current caught him and swirled him off his feet, but the wooden stool bobbed and floated on top of the water.

"*Oof!*" spluttered Tomkin, and he kicked and splashed until he and the stool were on the far side of the river. They staggered up the bank, and sat down to rest.

"You're a very good swimmer," Tomkin said to the three-legged stool. "And when I'm king I promise I'll make you prime minister."

The stool spun round on two legs and sang:

"Promises, promises, one, two, three,
A king will never remember me."

"Yes, I will," said Tomkin indignantly.

Tomkin and the stool walked on and on, and as they walked they noticed that the grass and bushes on either side of the path were dusty brown. The trees had no leaves and the earth was hard and cracked.

"It looks as if it hasn't rained here for ages and

ages," said Tomkin. "But it must be going to rain soon – look at the sky!"

The sky was leaden grey, and a huge black cloud was swirling round the top of the hill ahead of them. They could see a village halfway up the hill, and beyond the village was a castle.

"Maybe that's my kingdom," Tomkin said.

"Maybe it is," said the stool. "It certainly looks as if all the people have come out to meet us."

Tomkin stopped and stared. The three-legged stool was quite right – many men and women and children were hurrying down the hill towards them.

Tomkin shook his head. "I don't think I want to be king here," he said. "All these people look as sad as sad can be."

A bony little girl reached Tomkin and the three-legged stool first.

"Oh, please!" she gasped, clutching at Tomkin's arm. "Please – have you come to make it rain?"

"What?" Tomkin said. "What do you mean? There's the biggest blackest cloud I ever saw over there – it must be about to rain puddles and ponds and lakes and seas any moment now."

The little girl began to cry, although not one tear came out of her eyes. "But that's just it!" she wailed. "The cloud is always there – but it never, ever rains! All our rivers have dried up, and we've had no water now for days and weeks and months. Our cows and sheep have run away, and we have nothing left to eat but one cupful of flour. All our fields are dry and bare except for one small cabbage. And if it doesn't rain soon, we will all dry up into dust and blow away in the wind."

Tomkin looked around him at all the people. They were gazing at him, their eyes huge and hopeful in their thin pinched faces. He looked up at the black cloud, and he shifted his bag on his back and rubbed his nose.

"Well…" he said.

"Ahem," said the three-legged stool in a small voice beside him. "Doesn't that cloud look full of rain? As full of rain as a bag might be full of needles and reels of cotton … but one snip from your scissors and they'd all fall out!"

"*Oh!*" said Tomkin. "Oh, yes! How clever you are – when I'm king I'm certainly going to make you prime minister!"

The stool spun round on three legs and sang:

"Promises, promises, one, two, three,
A king will never remember me."

"Just you wait and see!" said Tomkin, and he marched on along the path and up the hill.

"Be careful!" the stool called after him. "A little can go a very long way!"

"I know what I'm doing," said Tomkin.

Up and up he went; past the village and past the castle until he was at the top of the hill and the huge black cloud was billowing just above his head. Tomkin swung the bag off his back and pulled out his scissors.

"Look at me!" he shouted.

Snip! Snap! Rip! Tomkin cut three long slashes right across the cloud. WHOOSH! the rush of rain washed him off his feet and sent him gasping and tumbling all the way back down to the bottom of the hill.

"HURRAH! HURRAH! HURRAH!" shouted the men and the women and the children, and they danced round and round in the silver sheets of pouring rain. They laughed and they sang and they cried and they cheered, and they picked up Tomkin and carried him back up the hill to the castle.

"You must be our king!" they said, and they sat him on a golden throne and put a golden crown on his head. They fetched him hot cabbage soup and soft white rolls, and they showed him his bed heaped with thick red blankets.

At the bottom of the hill the three-legged stool waited for Tomkin. It stood there with the rain beating down on it, and a cold wind blowing about it. In a small, sad voice it sang:

"Promises, promises, one, two, three,
When will the king remember me?"

It went on raining. It rained without stopping, day and night, night and day. The trees and the fields grew green, and then became dark and heavy with the never-ending rain. Up in the castle Tomkin laughed and danced and sang, but as the rains went on he watched the rivers begin to flow again, and then fill and fill until they flooded their banks and rushed and gushed all over the country-side. The men and the women and the children stopped being happy and began to complain.

"What's the use of rain if it never stops?" they asked each other. "We were unhappy before, but if the floods wash our village away we'll be even worse off." And they walked up the path to the castle and demanded to see King Tomkin.

"You must stop the rain and bring back the sun," they said. "If you can't, we'll take away your crown and send you off on your travels again."

"Oh, dear," said Tomkin. "Well – maybe I could sew the holes together."

He put his bag on his back and walked out of the castle and up to the top of the hill with the villagers following behind him. The black cloud was still in the sky, but it had poured out so much water that it was now high up, and far beyond his reach. Tomkin rubbed his nose.

"I need a ladder," he said. "I need lots of ladders."

"Then will you make it stop raining?" asked a little boy.

Tomkin nodded. "I'll try," he said.

"Hurrah!" shouted the little boy. "King Tomkin is going to mend the cloud!"

All the men and women and children from the village went hurrying off through the rain to fetch their ladders. They fetched their tables, and they fetched their chairs, and they heaped them one on top of the other into a tower that rose higher and higher.

"It's not high enough," Tomkin said. "What else have you got?"

They brought out beds and baths and chests of drawers. They carried dressers and cupboards and baskets and buckets and boxes, and piled them up and up.

"Is there anything else?" asked Tomkin.

"Nothing," said the villagers, staring at the tottering tower and shaking their dripping heads. "There's not so much as a bead box left to bring."

"All right," said Tomkin. "Now I'll see what I can do." And he began to climb.

Up went Tomkin, pulling himself up the ladders and climbing up and over the cupboards and chairs. Soon he could see the world around him for miles and miles, and still he climbed up and up. The big black cloud grew closer and closer, and he shook the rain from his eyes and kept on climbing.

Tomkin reached the top of the tower. He stood

on the highest chair and stretched upwards ... and he couldn't reach. He could see the three long splits in the cloud, but he was just too far away to touch them.

"I can't do it!" Tomkin said. "I can't reach."

The villagers began to whisper to each other and to mutter and to growl.

"Throw down your crown, Tomkin!" they shouted. "You're no king of ours! Throw down your crown, and be on your way!"

Tomkin looked down. He saw the cold, miserable villagers, and he saw that all their tables and chairs and cupboards and beds and boxes were wet and spoiled. He saw the rain-soaked fields, and the rippling floodwater creeping closer and closer to the village. And far, far off, at the bottom of the path, he saw the three-legged stool patiently waiting for him.

Tomkin took a deep breath. "I cut the cloud too deeply and I've made it rain for ever and ever," he said. "And I forgot my oldest friend. I don't deserve to be a king," and he tossed the crown to the ground. His tears dropped down and mixed with the streams of water flowing down the hill ... down to the three-legged stool.

Up jumped the stool, and hurried up the hill.

"Stop!" it called. "Wait for me!" And it scurried through the groups of wailing villagers to the bottom of the tower. Tomkin was sitting at the top with his head in his hands, but when he heard the stool calling he sat up straight and wiped his eyes.

Everyone watched the stool scrambling up the tower. Up and up it went, and when it reached the top Tomkin held it steady.

"I'm so sorry I forgot you," he said. "I truly am."

"No time for that now," said the stool as it balanced itself on top of the very topmost chair. "Come along – climb on me."

Tomkin took his needles and thread out of his bag, and climbed on the stool. He was just high enough to reach the three long rips in the cloud and he began to sew. He sewed all day long without stopping once, and gradually the rain grew less and less, until by the evening there was only a fine mist in the air.

"A couple more stitches and I'll be done," said Tomkin.

"That's good," said the stool.

Tomkin stopped suddenly.

"Oh!" he said. "Oh, no!"

"What's the matter?" asked the stool.

"It's no good," Tomkin said, "it's no good at all. There are needle holes in the cloud at the beginning and end of every stitch. I can see thousands of water drops squeezing through them – I'll *never* be able to stop the rain."

"Nobody wants you to stop the rain for ever," said the stool. "Finish your stitching."

"But it's no good," Tomkin said. "The whole village will be washed away, and it's all my fault." He made his last stitch and pulled it tight.

"Well done," said the stool. "Now look!"

Tomkin looked. The setting sun had come creeping out from behind the cloud and was shining through the mist. A rainbow was shimmering from one side of the hill to the other, and the puddles and ponds and lakes were shining golden mirrors of light.

"KING TOMKIN! KING TOMKIN!" called the villagers. "Come down and take up your crown!"

Tomkin shook his head, and began climbing down the tower with the three-legged stool close behind him. Halfway down, a gust of wind blew a flurry of raindrops against Tomkin's face.

"Why!" he said. "The rain's like silver needles! It

must be blowing through the needle holes in the cloud – but it isn't rushing and gushing like it was before."

"That's right," said the stool. "A little can go a very long way."

Tomkin reached the ground, picked up the crown and handed it to the oldest villager.

"I'm not fit to be a king," he said, "but if you want someone wise and clever I think you should ask the three-legged stool."

The villager bowed to the stool, and the stool bowed back.

"A king," said the stool, "should always know when he's made a mistake."

"Quite so," said the oldest villager.

"And a king should be willing to work all day without stopping for the good of his people," said the stool.

"My thoughts exactly," said the oldest villager.

"And a king should be as happy when he has nothing but a bag of needles as when he has a golden throne."

"I couldn't have put it better myself," said the oldest villager, and he picked up the golden crown and handed it back to Tomkin.

"Hurrah for King Tomkin!" shouted all the villagers.

Tomkin held up his hand and the men and the women and the children were silent.

"Thank you very much," he said, and he bowed. "But I will only be king if the three-legged stool is prime minister."

"It will be my pleasure," said the three-legged stool.

"Hurrah for the three-legged stool! Three cheers for our prime minister! And three more cheers for our wonderful king!" The villagers picked Tomkin up and carried him off to the castle.

The three-legged stool and the oldest villager walked up the path together.

"The best king of all," said the oldest villager, "is a king who keeps his promises."

And the stool sang:

"Promises, promises, one, two, three,
This is the king for you and me!"

and he followed Tomkin into the castle with a hop, a skip and a jump.

Little Beekeeper

Once in the time of wizards there was a wizard who had three sons and one daughter. The daughter was the youngest, and no one thought very much about her. All day long she washed the clothes and cooked the meals and cleaned the house, and every evening she ran up to the apple orchard to talk to the bees in their hives. When she came back to the house she sat and stitched and sewed in a corner of the kitchen and said almost nothing at all. Her brothers called her Little Beekeeper, and the wizard fell into the habit of doing the same.

The wizard's sons were fine and strong and handsome, but they hadn't an ounce of wizardry among them. They could cut down a tree with one swing of an axe, but they couldn't send thunderbolts hurling across the sky. They could carry enough logs on one shoulder to keep a grandmother warm all winter, but they couldn't turn the smallest prince into a toad. They could split branches into matchsticks with one hand tied behind their back, but they couldn't see faraway places in a bowl of magic water – all they could see was their own reflections, and very good-looking they thought themselves.

"Oh, dearie, dearie me!" said the wizard, and he looked at his three fine sons in despair. "Whatever will you do in life? I'm a wizard, and my father was a wizard … and I don't know anything about anything else!" And he went up into his tall tower room to think. Little Beekeeper ran to the apple orchard where the beehives were, and whispered and whispered at the door of each hive:

"My brothers are so strong and tall,
My father can't see me at all.
Bees, dear bees, I beg of you,
Tell me now what I must do!"

24

"Zzzzz! Zzzzz! Zzzzz!" buzzed the bees, and Little Beekeeper nodded and ran back home. She picked up her broom and began sweeping the hallway.

The wizard sat in his tower room with his head in his hands. He had made enchantments and experiments and magic of every kind; he was worn out by mixing and stirring and drawing secret signs at midnight in the sand of the forest floor. Nothing had worked; his three sons remained fine and strong and handsome, but nothing more.

The wizard sighed. "I'm growing old, and my magic is fading away. There's nothing more that I can do. They must go out into the world and seek their fortunes."

Bang! Bang! Bang! There was a loud knocking.

The wizard jumped up and hurried down the stairs. He pushed past Little Beekeeper and opened the door. Outside was a messenger dressed all in black, and when he saw the wizard he bowed low and handed him a letter.

"From the palace," he said, "to every household in the land."

Little Beekeeper stopped sweeping and listened.

The wizard took the letter eagerly, pulled his spectacles from his pocket and began to read.

"Dearie, dearie me," he said to himself as he read.

Whosoever can find their way to the Royal Castle and fill the Great Hall COMPLETELY AND ENTIRELY with whatsoever they pick and choose, leaving no nook or chink or cranny unfilled, shall rule the kingdom for ever and a day. BEWARE ~ those who fail will be thrown into the Deepest Darkest Dungeon

"The queen growing old and feeble? Dear, dear. And no prince or princess to rule the kingdom afterwards! Goodness gracious. And a competition – a competition to find a new king or queen from among the people... Well, well, *well!* Now, let me see..."

The wizard rubbed his hands together. "My boys are fine and strong and handsome. They could never fail." He folded up the letter and put it in his pocket as he went back up the stairs. Little Beekeeper went on sweeping the hallway, and she sang as she swept.

"Silence!" shouted the wizard from his tower room. Little Beekeeper stopped singing, but she smiled as she began to dust and polish.

When the three sons came rolling back from their game of skittles, the wizard told them about the competition.

"You are all strong and can work hard," he said. "Surely one of you can fill the queen's hall and become king of all the land? And then your brothers will be princes, and you will all live happily ever after."

Little Beekeeper listened as she stitched away at a pile of holey socks but she said nothing. Her three brothers laughed and joked and banged each other on the back.

"No one is as strong as us!" they boasted. "One of us will become king before the week is out!" Then they began to argue about which of them should go first, and what they would do as soon as they were made king. They argued so loudly and for so long that at last the wizard called up all his strength and sent a thunderbolt to silence them.

"I know!" shouted the youngest son as he picked himself up from the floor. "We'll ask Little Beekeeper who should go first!" And he pointed to his sister, sitting and sewing in her corner.

"She knows nothing about anything!" said the middle son. "Why, she's good for nothing but looking after the bees!"

"Then let her ask the bees which of us should go first!" said the oldest son, and he pulled Little Beekeeper out of her corner and pushed her out of the door. Up to the apple orchard she ran, and whispered and whispered at the door of each hive:

"Bees, dear bees, I beg of you,
Tell me now what I should do!"

"Zzzzz! Zzzzz! Zzzzz!" buzzed the bees. Little Beekeeper nodded. Then she hurried back to the kitchen.

"Well?" shouted her brothers. Little Beekeeper

pointed at the oldest.

"I said she was good for nothing," grumbled the middle brother.

"She's good for nothing at all," complained the youngest, but the oldest was already pulling on his coat.

The wizard's oldest son marched along the road to the queen's castle. As he went he swung his axe round and round his head and thought about how he would soon be king.

"I shall play skittles every day," he said to himself, "and my skittles will be made of silver." And he laughed as he strode up the steps to the castle door and banged on the knocker as loudly as he could.

The door was opened by a little old woman dressed all in black.

The oldest son looked her up and down. "When I live here," he announced, "I shall have soldiers dressed in red and purple to answer the door." And he pushed past the old woman and stared rudely about him.

"I've come to be king, old leatherface," he said.

"Show me the hall, and I'll fill it!"

The old woman smiled, and her little black eyes glittered and shone.

"Come this way, my young and foolish boy," she said, and she led the oldest son along a dark and winding corridor. At the end she threw open a heavy door studded with iron nails. The oldest son strode through, and then stopped. He was standing in the most enormous hall he had ever seen. It was truly vast. The soaring arched roof rose up and up and up above the dirty and flaking walls, and the blackened floor stretched away and away in front of him. The tall windows were coated with dust and laced with spiders' webs, and the light that came in was dim and grey.

"Oh," said the oldest son, looking all about him. "Ah."

"You have three days and three nights," said the old woman. "You may come and you may go for those three days and nights, but if at the end the great hall is not filled completely and entirely, every nook and chink and cranny, then you will be thrown into the deepest dungeon for ever and ever and ever." And she turned round and shuffled away.

The oldest son shook himself. "Well," he said,

"I'd be better beginning than standing here and staring. After all, I can cut down a tree with one swing of my axe. I'll soon have this hall filled completely and entirely." He rushed out of the hall and back the way he had come. He burst out of the castle door, and as he hurried into the forest he was already swinging his axe above his head. He chose the tallest tree and felled it with one blow.

"H'mph," he said to himself as he hauled and heaved the tree-trunk round the corners of the corridor. "When I am king I'll have this castle pulled right down and build myself a marvellous and magnificent palace." And he pulled the tree into the hall and went back for another, and another, and another.

At the end of the three days and nights the oldest son had filled the great hall. Tree-trunks were heaped high and branches and twigs piled above them, up to the arches of the roof. Leaves littered the floor. The oldest son lay, puffing and panting, in the doorway.

The old woman came shuffling up.

"Well, well, well," she said. "So you think you

31

have filled the hall completely and entirely?"

"That I have, old bag and baggage," said the oldest son. "Now, give me my crown!"

"Not so fast," said the old woman, and she clapped her hands. A flock of white pigeons came fluttering all around her, cooing and clucking and murmuring.

"Fly, my little dears!" the old woman told them. "Fly! Find me any nooks and chinks and crannies!"

The pigeons flapped their wings and rose up into the air like a scattering of white petals. They flew in and out of the tree-trunks, they perched among the branches, they paddled up and down among the leaves.

"Ho, ho, ho!" The old woman cackled delightedly. "No crown for you, my fine and foolish fellow!" And she clapped her hands a second time. The pigeons swooped down and touched her cheek with their soft wings, and then fluttered away. As they left the hall there was the crunch of marching feet. Six silver soldiers came wheeling round from the corridor. They seized the oldest son as if he weighed less than a feather, and although he struggled and shouted they carried him off and away down to the deepest dungeon in the castle.

As the heavy wooden door swung shut there was a flash and a bang. A wisp of purple smoke floated up. The oldest son felt himself shrinking and shrinking, and his skin wrinkled and turned greenish yellowish brown. He tried to shout for help.

"Croak! Croak! Croak!" was all he could say. "Croak! Croak! Croak!"

No one answered, and he was left with a heap of wet hay to sleep under and a crust of bread to eat.

The old wizard, the two remaining brothers and Little Beekeeper waited and waited for the oldest son to come marching home in triumph. At last the wizard shook his head and went to try his spells over a bowl of magic water. *Abracadabra*! There was the deepest darkest dungeon of the castle, and there was the oldest son's coat hanging on a rusty nail. *Fsss-sss-ss*! The picture clouded over.

"Oh dear me," said the wizard. "My poor, poor boy! Will we ever see him again?"

The second brother snorted. "Serves him right. Now it's *my* turn to go. I'll be crowned king before the end of the week!" He pulled on his hat, snatched up his axe and set out along the road, whistling and singing as he went.

"When I am king," he said to himself, "I shall play skittles every day, and my skittles will be made of solid gold."

The second son knocked on the castle door, and the old woman dressed all in black opened it.

"*Well!*" said the second son, staring at her. "When I am king the door will be opened by a string of servants, all dressed in scarlet silks and satins. Show me the great hall, old raggletaggle. I have come to be made king!"

The old woman smiled, and her little black eyes glittered and shone.

"Come with me," she said, "my young and foolish boy," and she led him along the winding passage to the great hall.

The hall was empty and echoing. The second son looked all around him, his eyes popping wide with amazement.

"You have three days and three nights," said the old woman. "You may come and you may go for those three days and nights, but if at the end the great hall is not filled completely and entirely, every nook and chink and cranny, then you will be thrown into the deepest dungeon for ever and ever and ever." And she turned round and shuffled away.

The second son rubbed his head. "I'd best get busy," he said to himself, and he shouldered his axe and hurried outside. At the edge of the forest he stopped. In front of him was a mighty heap of tree-trunks and branches and twigs and leaves, piled high and seeming to reach almost to the sky.

"This looks like my brother's work," said the second son, "and very handy it will be!" And he began to chop the tree-trunks and branches into logs. When he had built a stack he swung them onto his shoulder and carried them into the great hall. In two days and nights he had used up all the wood his brother had cut, and he hastily cut more and more and more from the forest trees. At the end of three days and nights the great hall was filled to the very rafters, and the second brother lay puffing and panting in the doorway.

The old woman came shuffling up.

"Well, well, well," she said. "So you think you have filled the hall completely and entirely?"

"Can't you see that I have, old tortoise?" said the second son. "Bring me my crown!"

"Not so fast," said the old woman, and she clapped her hands. A drift of butterflies came floating down around her, their wings shining in the dim and dusty air.

"Go, my pretties!" The old woman waved them towards the logs. "See if you can find me any nooks and chinks and crannies!"

The butterflies flew up and up and up. They flittered in and out between the logs, and they settled and opened and closed their bright wings in every space.

"Ho, ho, ho!" The old woman shook with laughter. "No crown for you, my fine and foolish fellow!" And again she clapped her hands. The butterflies drifted away, brushing her cheeks with their painted wings as they went. The six silver soldiers came marching down the corridor. The second son found himself picked up as if he weighed nothing at all. In no time he was bundled into the deepest darkest dungeon.

As the heavy wooden door swung shut there was a flash and a bang. A wisp of orange smoke floated up. The second son felt himself shrinking and shrinking, and his skin wrinkled and turned greenish yellowish brown.

"Croak! Croak!" said a large fat toad in the corner.

The second son looked up. "Croak," he said, and he hopped across to steal the crust of bread.

The old wizard, the third son and Little Beekeeper waited and waited for the second son to come marching home in triumph. At last the wizard sighed and went to look in his bowl of magic water. The water was misty and cloudy, and the wizard groaned.

"My magic is all used up!" he said, but as he muttered spell after spell the water slowly cleared. *Abracadabra*! There was the oldest son's coat still hanging on the dungeon wall, and there beside it was the second son's hat.

"Poor, poor boys," said the wizard sadly.

"My turn now!" said the youngest son. "I'm *sure* to be made king! I'm the finest, the strongest, the handsomest of us all!" And he tucked his axe into his belt and set off along the road, humming cheerfully.

"When I'm king," he said to himself, "I shall play skittles all day with a ball made of diamonds and rubies!"

The youngest son knocked so hard on the castle door that sparks flew in the air.

"You'll have to be off, old brittlebones," he told the old woman in black. "I'm to be king here, and I'll have knights in golden armour to open the door for me. Now, take me to the hall!"

The old woman led the youngest son down the long winding corridor. She smiled as she walked in front of him, and her little black eyes glittered and shone.

"You have three days and three nights," she told him. "You may come and you may go for those three days and nights, but if at the end the great hall is not filled completely and entirely, every nook and chink and cranny, then you will be thrown into the deepest dungeon for ever and ever and ever." And she turned round and shuffled away.

The youngest son hardly listened. He was pacing

out the length and the width of the floor, and squinting up into the dusty arched roof.

"H'mph!" he said. "It'll be hard work, but it can be done!" And when he found the enormous heap of logs at the edge of the forest he nodded. "Just what I need!" he said, and set to work splitting them into the finest of matchsticks.

As the three days and nights went by, the youngest son worked faster and faster. He ran to and fro filling the hall with armfuls of matchsticks. At the last minute he pushed the final sliver of wood into place.

"Not a chink or a nook or a cranny that isn't filled!" he gasped, and fell down in the doorway puffing and panting.

"We'll see about that," said the old woman as she shuffled up beside him. "We'll see!" and she clapped her hands.

A black wave of tiny ants came flooding down the corridor. The old woman nodded to them.

"My tiny ones, creep and climb and crawl! Find all the nooks and chinks and crannies!"

The ants scattered in among the matchstick slivers of wood. They crept and they climbed and they crawled in among the nooks and the chinks and the crannies, and the old woman rocked with laughter.

"Ho, ho, ho! No crown for you, my fine and foolish fellow!" And she clapped her hands together until all the ants had crawled back through the wooden matchsticks and were gathered at her feet. They swirled around her, and then scurried away as the six silver soldiers came marching up the corridor.

As the heavy wooden door swung shut on the youngest son there was the brightest flash of all. A cloud of green smoke floated up, and the youngest son coughed as he felt himself shrinking and shrinking.

"Croak! Croak! Croak!" said the two fat toads in the corner, and they watched as the youngest son's skin wrinkled and turned greenish yellowish brown. The youngest son tried to cough again, but he could only croak. He sat and glared angrily at the two fat toads, and they glared back. On the dungeon wall the youngest son's belt hung beside the coat and the hat.

The old wizard and Little Beekeeper waited and waited for the youngest son to come marching home in triumph. The wizard peered into his bowl of magic water, but it was green and weedy and he could see nothing at all.

"My poor, poor boys," he said, and he sighed heavily. "Will I ever see them again?"

Little Beekeeper stood up. "Now, Father," she said, "it is my turn to go to the castle."

"*You?*" said the wizard. "What can *you* do?" And he went up into his tall tower room to stare sadly out over the forest.

Little Beekeeper smiled, but she said nothing. She picked up a plate, a spoon and a basket and went out to the apple orchard. When she came back the plate was heaped with honeycomb, and the basket was full of beeswax. She covered the honey with a cloth, and for the rest of the day she cleaned and softened and smoothed the wax. When the evening star began to climb the pale silver sky she pulled three long hairs from her head, and twisted and plaited them together. As the moon followed the star up and up into the

41

velvet night Little Beekeeper spun the soft yellow wax round and round and round the twist of hair, until by the time the moon sank down once more at the other end of night she had made a tall and golden candle.

As the sun rose, Little Beekeeper knocked on her father's door.

"Father," she said, "I've come to say goodbye."

The wizard stroked his beard. "Don't go, Little Beekeeper," he said. "Who will wash the clothes and cook the meals and clean the house? Don't go."

Little Beekeeper shook her head. "The bees are waiting to show me the way." She ran down the stairs and into the kitchen. She picked up the plate of honeycomb and carefully wrapped the tall golden candle in her shawl. Outside the door the bees were buzzing and humming in a quivering cloud, and as Little Beekeeper stepped out they flew up into the air and led her away down the path through the forest.

When Little Beekeeper reached the castle she climbed slowly up the steps and knocked gently at the door. The bees flew high in the air as the old woman dressed all in black came out. Little

Beekeeper curtsied down to the ground, and held out the plate of honey.

"Madam," she said, "I bring you a present."

The old woman smiled, and her eyes were bright and shining.

"Thank you, my child," she said. "Will you rest a little after your journey?"

Little Beekeeper curtsied again. "If you please, I should like to see the great hall."

The old woman took Little Beekeeper by the hand and led her down the long winding corridor into the vast and empty cavern of the hall.

"You have three days and three nights, my dear. You may come and you may go for those three days and nights, but if at the end the great hall is not filled completely and entirely, every nook and chink and cranny, then you will be thrown into the deepest dungeon for ever and ever and ever. But, dear child, why don't you run away home and be safe for ever and a day?"

Little Beekeeper touched her arm gently. "Thank you," she said, "but I must stay."

The old woman nodded, and shuffled away.

As soon as the old woman had gone, Little

43

Beekeeper looked all around her. She saw the cob-webs and the flaking walls and the dim grey light. Then she sat down on the blackened and dirty floor in the very centre of the hall, her shawl in her lap. There she sat, for three days and three nights. Every night at midnight the old woman came and asked if there was anything she wished for, but Little Beekeeper only smiled and shook her head.

At midnight on the third night the castle bell tolled twelve long strokes. There was no glimmer of light coming through the tall dusty windows, and the great hall was as black as night's own shadow. Little Beekeeper stirred, and stood up. She unwrapped the tall golden candle and placed it on the floor. She took a tinderbox from her pocket, struck a spark and lit the candle. The flame flick-ered for a moment, and then burnt straight and tall and golden. Light welled up, and the darkness fled away. The whole of the great hall glowed warm and yellow like molten gold.

Little Beekeeper walked slowly to the iron studded door and opened it. The old woman was standing on the other side. As she saw the great hall filled with light, she cried out and clapped her hands.

At once a swarm of bees came buzzing and humming and bumbling all about her.

"Fly, fly, my precious ones," said the old woman. "Fly and search the great hall. See if it is filled completely and entirely."

The bees flew up and around the hall. They flew this way and that, they flew high and they flew low, but wherever they flew the golden light of Little Beekeeper's candle shone.

"Zzzzz! Zzzzz! Zzzzz!" buzzed the bees, and they circled round Little Beekeeper's head.

"Every nook and chink and cranny is full of light," said the old woman. "At last the great hall is filled, completely and entirely." And she clapped her hands one last time.

Six silver soldiers came marching, marching down the long winding corridor. They were carrying cloaks of silk and satin and velvet, and a crown of silver and gold glittering with diamonds and rubies. The old woman swung one cloak round her own shoulders, and the other she wrapped around Little Beekeeper. She took the crown, and placed it on Little Beekeeper's head.

"Be queen, my dear," she said, "and be happy."

There was a roaring of trumpets and a crashing of drums. Suddenly the great hall was filled with people, all cheering for their new queen. The floor was polished silver, and the walls were shining gold, and diamonds twinkled in the glittering arches of the roof. At the end of the hall was a golden throne studded with rubies, and the old queen took Little Beekeeper by the hand and led her to her rightful place.

And what happened then? What of the wizard and the three brothers?

The feasting and rejoicing went on for days and days and days, but the brothers and the wizard knew nothing about it. At last a messenger arrived at the wizard's house, carefully carrying a bowl of water.

"A gift from the queen, sire," he said.

The wizard took the bowl and peered into it. He saw a picture in its clear depths, a picture of Little Beekeeper dressed in royal robes and wearing a gold and silver crown. He saw her raise her hand and send a thunderbolt flashing up and up into the roof of the great hall. It exploded with a crash,

Under the Moon

Once upon a time there was a little old woman and a little old man who lived together in a little old house. They would have been very happy but for one thing: the little old woman just could not sit still. Never ever did she sit down and share a cup of cocoa with the little old man. Dust dust dust, polish polish polish, shine shine shine – all day long she was busy.

The little old man began to sigh, and to grow lonely. While their ten tall children were growing up in their neat little house he didn't have time to notice how the little old woman never stopped working. Now, however, he liked to sit by the fire and dream, and he thought it would be a friendly thing if the little old woman sat beside him.

"You could knit a little knitting," said the little old man, "or sew a little seam?"

But the little old woman said, "No, no, no! I must dust and sweep and clean."

The little old man sighed a long sad sigh and went and put the kettle on. He sat down beside the fire with Nibbler the dog and Plum the cat, and Nibbler curled up at his feet and Plum curled up on his lap, but still the little old man felt lonely.

The little old woman went on sweeping the yard with her broom, even though the stars were beginning to twinkle in the sky.

One day there was a knocking on the door.

"Who's there?" asked the little old woman, running to open the door with her duster in one hand and her mop in the other.

"It's me," said young Sally from the cottage down the road. "My mum says you'm the bestest cleaner in all the village, and we've just got two new babies as like as two peas, and all the children running here and there with smuts on their noses and dirt on their toeses, and our mum was a-wondering...?"

The little old woman didn't wait another moment. She picked up her broom as she ran through the door, and she fairly flew down the road to Sally's cottage. All day she polished and swept and scrubbed, and by the time the stars were twinkling the cottage down the road was as shiny as a new pin; as fresh as a daisy; as polished as a one minute chestnut fallen from the tree.

"Well, well, well," said the little old man as she hurried through the door. "There's a good day's work you've done. Would you like a little cocoa?"

The little old woman actually sat down.

"Thank you kindly, my dear," she said. "Just a sip or two – and then I must polish our own little house." And she sat quietly beside the little old man for five minutes.

"This is fine and dandy," said the little old man, smiling. Nibbler laid his head on the little old woman's feet, and Plum purred happily.

"Just as it should be of a gentle summer evening," said the little old man.

"No, no, no!" said the little old woman. She drank the last drop of her cocoa and jumped to her feet. "It was very nice, but I must hurry hurry hurry." And she seized the duster and hurried off to the dresser full of china to polish and shine. The little old man sighed, but it was a medium-sized sigh.

"Five minutes is five minutes more than nothing," he said. Nibbler nodded his head.

The next day brought another knocking on the door.

"Who's there?" said the little old woman, running to the door with her dustpan in one hand and a broom in the other.

"It is I," said the parson from the church across the hill. "I have heard that you are the most wonderful cleaner in the county, and my church is full of mice and moths and mildew."

The little old woman jumped to her feet. She picked up her soap and a bucket as she ran through the door, and she hurried and scurried to the church across the hill. She swept and she dusted and she rubbed, and by the end of the day the church was glowing as if a hundred candles had been lit inside.

"Well, well, well," said the little old man as she walked through the door. "There's another good day's work done. Could you fancy a cup of cocoa?"

"Thank you kindly," said the little old woman, and she sat down on the bench by the fire with a flop.

"Just a small cup, and then I must scrub our own back yard." But she sat quietly with the little old man and with Nibbler the dog and Plum the cat for ten long minutes. Then up she hopped and away she went with the broom in the yard.

The little old man sighed a very little sigh.

"What do you think, Nibbler? Isn't ten minutes ten whole minutes more than nothing?"

Nibbler nodded, and Plum purred.

The next day no one came to the house. The little old woman cleaned and rubbed and scrubbed her little house inside and out, and when the stars began to twinkle in the bluebell sky she was still swishing her soapsuds in the tub. Then there came a knock at the door – such a timid, quiet little knock you could hardly hear it. The little old woman hurried to see who it was, her hands wet and dripping.

"Who's there?" she asked.

Standing on the doorstep was a strange grey shadow of a man. His hair was long and silver, and his clothes were all a-tremble about him.

"I hear," he whispered in a voice as soft as a bird's breath, "that you are the very best cleaner in all the ups and downs of the Earth?"

The little old woman nodded briskly. She shook the water from her hands, and the drops flew through the air.

"How can I help you?" she asked.

"It's the cobwebs," said the silvery grey person. "I don't know what to do about them."

The little old woman ran back into the house and picked up her broom and a basket of dusters.

"Just tell me where they are," she said fiercely. "I've never met a cobweb yet that didn't whisk away when I got busy."

The silvery grey person waved his arms in the air, and silver dust scattered about him.

"Up there," he whispered, "seventeen times as high as the moon."

The little old woman looked up into the night sky. Sure enough, there, high above the moon, were long trails of cobweb lying across the sky. She hurried inside, and shook the little old man from his doze in front of the rosy crackling fire.

"Come along, my dear," she said, "I need your help."

Nibbler and Plum ran out with the little old man, but when Nibbler saw the stranger he began to whine. He lowered his head, and crawled back into the house with his tail tucked under him. Plum was not afraid. She greeted the grey person as an old friend, purring and rubbing in and out of his legs.

"Whatever is it?" asked the little old man.

"We need your help," said the little old woman. She shook the dusters out of the basket, and settled herself and her broom inside.

"Now, my dear, toss me up, just as high as ever you can."

The little old man picked up the basket. He shut his eyes and counted to three. Then, with a heave and a pitch and a toss, he threw the little old woman up and up and up into the air. Up she flew, higher and higher, until the little old man could only see her as a tiny speck against the light of the moon.

The silvery grey stranger bowed a long and quivery bow.

"I do thank you," he said in his soft thread of a voice, and he shook himself all over. Silvery sparkles flew in the air and settled on the little old man and on the ground around him; it made the old man sneeze – once, twice, three times.

When he had stopped sneezing the stranger was gone – flown back to his home in the moon. Looking up, the old man could see his pale face smiling down.

*　　*　　*

The little old woman came back with the sunlight in the early morning. She slept a little in her rocking chair, and then bustled about the house. It seemed to the little old man that she was not as quick as usual.

When evening came the little old man put on the kettle, and sat down in front of the fire. Nibbler and Plum sat down with him, and so did the little old woman.

"That's a fine night's work," said the little old man, looking up into the clear and starlit sky. "Not a trace of a cobweb can I see."

The little old woman sniffed. "Indeed, I should hope not, my dear," she said. "When has a cobweb ever been too much for me and my broom? I shall be up again next full moon, just to make sure."

"Would you like a little cup of cocoa?" the little old man asked.

"Indeed I would, my dear," said the little old woman. "And, if it's all the same to you, I'll just sit quietly here this evening. It's tiring work, sweeping all those cobwebs away."

The little old man and the little old woman sat happily together. Nibbler slept curled up at their feet, and

Plum settled himself on the little old woman's lap.

It was the same the next night and every night until the full moon rose, and then once more the little old woman seated herself in her basket and the little old man tossed her up into the sky.

"Wheeeee!" she called, as she flew up and up and up. "Can you see me, my dear?"

"I can see you," the little old man said, smiling.

"Will you come with me next time the moon is full?" asked the little old woman.

"No, not I," said the little old man, and he went into the house as the little old woman flew up and away out of sight.

I'll sit by myself tonight, he thought as he put wood on the fire and the kettle on to boil, but she'll be here tomorrow and every night before the next full moon.

Up in the sky the little old woman was sweeping away the cobwebs. Down below the little old man was rocking in his chair, while the kettle bubbled happily on the hearth. The man in the moon smiled at them both, and the silver moon-sparkles glistened and shone in the little old man's hair. Nibbler and Plum slept peacefully, and there was not so much as the smallest of sighs in the little old house under the moon.

The Thistle Princess

Long, long ago, before time was caught and kept in clocks, there lived a king and a queen. They ruled their kingdom wisely and well, but they did not often smile. Sometimes the king would look out of the window and sigh, and sometimes the queen would sit under the willow tree in the royal garden and cry until the grass around her was wet with tears.

"Why is she crying?" whispered the roses.

"We don't know," murmured the lilies and poppies and daisies.

The willow shook his leafy head. "Why does the king sit and sigh?" he asked. "Who knows? Not I."

A small thistle was growing close by, hidden

among the willow's arching roots.

She shook her purple head and sniffed. "How silly they are," she said to herself. "It comes of being so beautiful. They've got no sense, no sense at all. Anyone sensible could see that the king and queen want a baby, a child, a little boy or girl to run about and laugh and keep them company from daybreak to sunset. Fiddlesticks!"

And she sniffed again. If the willow heard her, he took no notice. He was not in the habit of talking to thistles.

One day the gardener brought his youngest son to play in the garden.

"Excuse me for bringing him, Your Majesty," the gardener said, "but he'd like to see the flowers. He'll be no trouble."

The queen looked at the gardener's son and smiled. "He is most welcome," she said. "Everyone is welcome here."

And all day she watched the little boy as he toddled this way and that, up and down the paths and in and out of the roses and lilies and poppies and daisies.

The king, sitting at his window, watched as well

and he never sighed, not once.

"There!" said the little thistle, and she nodded to herself. "What have I been saying all along? What they need is a child of their own."

That evening, as the stars were creeping up the sky, the willow rustled his leaves.

"Ahem," he said, and the roses opened their sleepy eyes. The lilies lifted their heavy heads, and the poppies whispered, "Wake up! Wake up!" to the daisies.

"Ahem," said the willow, "I know now why the king and queen are so sad."

The flowers murmured and swayed.

"They are sad," the willow said, "because they have no children. While the gardener's child was here, the queen was happy all day and the king waved and smiled from his window."

The roses nodded. "We saw," they said. "But what can we do?"

The willow swept his long green fingers across the ground.

"There is nothing we can do. Nothing ... nothing ... nothing ..." And he swayed and sighed, and the roses and lilies and poppies and daisies swayed and sighed with him.

61

The little thistle could bear it no longer.

"Never mind about nothings," she said. "What a willow is good for is baskets. Forget fancy words, old man willow – weave a fine cradle for the king and the queen, and then we'll see what we can do."

There was a rustling and fluttering of leaves and twigs and branches.

"A weed!" trembled the roses. "A weed telling us what to do!"

The lilies drew back in alarm, and the poppies closed up their petals tightly. The willow quivered with indignation. Only the daisies looked at the thistle with their bright eyes and nodded to her. "A child?" they asked. "Can it be done?"

"It can!" said the thistle sternly. "Now, old man willow, are you all puff and pother and words, or are you willing to help that poor lonely king and queen?"

The willow took a moment or two to decide. To be ordered about by a common thistle was a dreadful thing, but not to help the king and queen of all the kingdom was surely worse...

Slowly the willow bowed his great green head, and his slender branches began to twist and weave, in and out and out and in.

"That's better," said the thistle, and she turned to the beds of flowers. "Come along! We need help from all of you."

As the willow laid the green leafy cradle on the grass, the roses leant gently over it and dropped pink and white and deep crimson petals inside. The lilies gave their golden fragrance, the poppies their crumpled scarlet silk, and the daisies shook in a scatter of bright whiteness.

"H'mph!" The willow turned to the thistle. "I hope you have no intention of adding your sharp needles and pins!"

The thistle sighed. "There has to be more than pretty leaves and petals," she said.

The little thistle waited until the flowers slept and the night was still. Then, slowly and painfully, she pulled up her roots from the warm earth and lay down in the willow cradle. She could feel herself wilting and shrivelling as she sank down into the soft petals. Her strong grey-green leaves withered and grew brittle, and her fine purple head turned to silver white.

"What needs doing must be done," she said, and she never spoke again.

The willow was woken in the morning by a strange sound. It was coming from the cradle, and he peered through his long green fingers in amazement. There, lying in the basket of his own making, was a baby – a baby with the skin of rose petals and the sweetness of lilies, and bright eyes that shone as she gazed up into the leaves above. She was wrapped in scarlet silk, and she kicked her little fat legs and laughed.

The queen was the next to hear the baby. She came running down the path, her arms outstretched. The king was close behind. Together they lifted the baby from the cradle and hugged her and loved her.

"Our very own baby!" whispered the queen.

"Our own princess!" smiled the king.

"There!" said the willow to the roses and lilies and poppies and daisies. "See how happy they are?" And he rustled his leaves proudly.

The king and queen carried the baby tenderly into the palace.

"Now that we have our hearts' desire," said the queen, "we must keep her safe from harm."

"Indeed we must!" said the king, and he gave

orders that a fence should be built around the royal garden to keep the baby princess safe. The baby waved her little arms and cried, but the king and queen took no notice.

Children came to stare at the fence. Then the gardener's little boy wriggled in between the bars and the other children followed him. They danced and sang to the baby princess, and she clapped her hands and laughed.

Autumns and winters came and went, and the baby grew into a little girl. The king and queen loved her so dearly that they spent every second of every minute of every hour watching over her.

"She is so beautiful!" smiled the queen. "She has skin as soft as rose petals."

"She smells as sweet as the golden lilies." laughed the king. "And her eyes are as lovely as the darkness in the hearts of poppies, and as bright as the eyes of daisies."

"She is our hearts' delight," said the queen, "and nothing and nobody must ever hurt her."

And she and the king gave orders that the fence should be taken down and replaced by a high wall with an iron gate. The princess ran to the gate and pulled at it. "No!" she called. "No!"

But the king ordered that it should stay.

The children waved to the princess through the gate. Then the gardener's youngest son showed them how to climb on each others' backs all the way up to the top of the wall, and they hopped down into the garden.

The children played hide-and-seek and catch-as-catch-can with the princess, and she skipped and jumped and ran with them all day and every day.

Springs and summers came and went. The princess went on growing, and the garden grew too. More and more flowers sprang up and flourished, and the royal garden became the wonder of the land.

The princess and the gardener's boy walked hand in hand under the arches of pink and white and deep crimson roses, and whispered with the other children among the golden lilies. The poppies dropped their scarlet petals and the daisies nodded and looked on with their bright eyes. The king and queen watched the princess and the children playing together and they shook their heads.

"Our daughter is so precious. What if she caught a cold, a mump or a measle from the outside children? We must protect her from all danger."

Orders were given to build another, higher wall. Iron spikes were placed on the top, and the gates were protected with the strongest steel bars.

"Please let my friends come in," begged the princess. "Please let them come and play!"

But the queen and the king only patted her and smiled fondly at her.

"Sit with me under the willow," said the queen, "and I will sing to you."

"Walk with me in the garden," invited the king, "and I will tell you stories of long ago."

The princess looked at them. "No," she said. "No." And she went to sit curled up in the branches of the willow, and slow silver tears ran down her cheeks.

The king and queen sighed, but they told each other it was all for the best.

"Could we ever forgive ourselves if she came to any harm?" asked the king.

"She is our everything," said the queen.

Outside the children gathered around the gates, but the guards ordered them to go home.

The gardener's youngest son struggled to climb the wall, but it was too high.

Suns and moons rose and set, and the princess grew tall and thin. She was pale now, and spent most of her days sitting beneath the willow tree, listening to the murmuring of the leaves.

"How right we were to keep those noisy children out of our garden," said the queen.

"Indeed," said the king. "They were far too rough. See how delicate and tender our princess is. She is safe here in our beautiful garden. We must make it as lovely as we can to give her pleasure."

Orchards were planted, full of sweet russet apples, velvet-skinned peaches and dusky plums. Fountains sparkled and waterfalls tumbled, and in the branches of the trees, gold and silver birds fluttered their shining wings. The princess grew still more pale and sad. Sometimes she walked among the roses and lilies and poppies and daisies and sighed, and sometimes she sat under the willow tree and cried until the ground was wet with tears.

Outside the walls the children lived their lives, but they seldom laughed or danced or sang. The gardener's youngest son often sat outside the gates, and one or other of the children would come and sit with him. They would speak quietly of the time long ago when they had played in the garden.

The king and queen walked under the trees with the princess.

"Look at the wonderful fountains!" the queen said.

"My friends would love to splash in the sparkling water," said the princess.

"No, no!" said the king. "Listen to the birds!"

"My friends would love to see them fly with their gold and silver wings," said the princess.

"No, no!" said the queen. The princess sighed and was silent. The king suddenly stopped.

"Look!" he said, and he pointed an angry finger. "Look! In our beautiful garden! A weed!"

"What is it?" The queen hurried to see. "Is it harmful? Will it hurt our darling?"

"It's a thistle," said the king. "Call for the gardeners! At once!"

The gardeners were called for. The thistle was taken away, but soon there was another, and then another. Professors and experts came from far and wide to give their opinion, but whatever they suggested it seemed that there were always more thistles. Thistles grew among the roses and lilies;

they grew among the poppies and daisies, and every day there were more and more and more.

"Whatever shall we do?" asked the king. "Our beautiful garden will soon be filled with thistles!"

At the steel-barred gate the gardener's youngest son was pleading with the guards.

"Let us in!" he begged. "Let us in, and we will pick the thistles. We ask no reward. Only let us into the garden and all the thistles will be gone."

The king and the queen looked up at each other.

"Did you hear?" asked the king.

The queen nodded.

"Children have bright eyes," said the king. "They will spy out even the smallest thistles. They can see things we cannot."

"That is true," said the queen, and she looked towards the willow tree. The princess was curled up in the branches, fast asleep.

She's as light as down, the old willow thought to himself, as light as thistledown.

The queen sighed.

"Our darling is so pale and sad. Maybe if the children pick the thistles she will smile again."

The king stood up: "Open the gates!"

70

As the gates opened, the children came dancing in. They skipped and hopped and ran all over the garden, picking every thistle they found. They skipped among the roses and lilies and poppies and daisies, and they picked big thistles and little thistles. They hopped among the apple trees, and peaches and plums, and they picked tall thistles and small thistles. They laughed as they ran in and out and round about the royal garden, and the king and queen smiled as they watched them.

"They look so happy," said the queen. "And look, the thistles are almost gone! And no more are growing!"

The king stroked his beard. "Perhaps," he said slowly, "perhaps we were wrong to build the wall. How long is it since we heard laughter in the garden?"

The queen didn't answer. She had run to help a very small boy who had fallen among the poppies.

She picked him up and he smiled at her. "Thank you," he said.

The queen's eyes filled with tears. "Oh," she said. "Oh … and we shut them out."

The king shook his head. "We were wrong. Our princess is our hearts' delight, but these are our children too. The children of our kingdom."

The queen put her hand on the king's shoulder.

"How wise," she said. "We must order the wall to be pulled down."

The gardener's youngest son came walking towards the king and the queen, and bowed.

"If you please," he said, "there are no more thistles. Do you wish us to leave now?"

The queen curtsied. "No," she said, "we would be honoured if you would stay."

The king turned to the guards. "As soon as you can," he ordered, "pull down the wall!"

The children laughed and danced round and round the king and queen. "Hurrah!" they shouted.

The gardener's son bowed once more. "And now," he said, "may we play with the princess?"

"Run to the willow and tell her that you may," said the queen, and the children ran with outstretched arms.

"Princess!" They called from under the tree. Up in the willow's branches the princess stirred in her sleep. "Come and play, Princess! We can play in the garden with you!"

"At last," whispered the princess.

Slowly she floated upwards, up and up through the whispering leaves. "Princess!" the children called again. "Where are you? Where are you?"

The gardener's son rubbed his eyes. Had he truly seen the princess drifting away into the evening shadows? He rubbed his eyes again and said nothing.

The king and queen ran to the tree and stared and stared up into the branches. There was nothing to be seen and nothing to be heard, except for the soft whispering and rustling of the leaves. The waiting children looked at them expectantly. "Is she asleep?" "Is she playing hide-and-seek?" The king shook his head. "We found her under the willow tree when she was a baby," he said sadly, "and now she has gone."

The queen put out her hand. "You are our children," she said.

"Now and for ever and ever," said the king.

As the shadows grew longer, the old willow sighed. "Willows weave beautiful cradles, but I will never weave again."

A very small thistle growing under the willow's roots sniffed loudly. "Fiddlesticks!" she said.

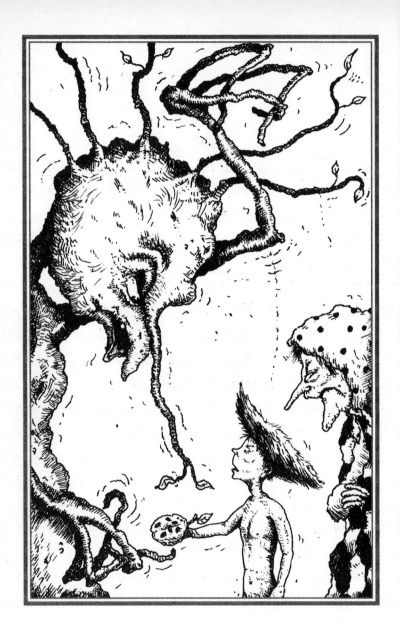

The Apple Child

There was once a cold village on the side of a tall cold mountain. Behind the village was a stony field where a flock of thin sheep huddled together under the shadow of a few spindly apple trees, and high above the mountain hung the moon; a pale cold moon that sent long dark shadows sprawling along the ground, creeping in and out of the village, and crouching down beside Ben's small cold cottage.

"*Brrrr*," shivered Ben, pulling an old sack round his shoulders. A little fire flickered in the grate, but there was no more wood left in the broken basket by the chimney. He got up and stared out of the window. Up on the mountainside he could see the apple trees quivering in the wind.

"I'll run up and see if there are any twigs or sticks under the trees," said Ben. He wrapped the sack more closely about himself, and slipped out of the cottage and up the street. The wind caught him and tugged and pulled at him, but he put his head down and trudged on to where the cold bare fields lay beyond the last house.

The sheep shifted unwillingly as Ben walked among them; "Saaaad," they bleated, "saaad!" The trees were moaning and muttering to each other, the wind snapped at their branches and whipped their last few leaves off and away.

High in the sky the moon gazed down. Ben glanced up, and for a moment he thought he saw a watching silver face.

"What can I do, Moon?" he called. "I'm cold – I'm ever so cold!"

There was no answer from the moon, but the wind suddenly dropped. Just for a moment there was a stillness, a silence as if all the moonlit world was holding its breath. Only a moment it lasted, and then up sprang the wind with a howl and a shriek, and tore the sack from Ben's back. The trees bent and swayed, and with a loud crash a long branch fell to the ground beside him.

"Thank you! Thank you!" Ben shouted, and he picked up the branch and ran as fast as he could back to his small cold cottage. The fire was a mere glimmer, but as he fed it first the smallest twig and then the bigger ones, it began to take heart and to glow warmly. Breaking the branch, he built the fire up higher, until the shadows were dancing and the smell of apple wood filled the room.

"*Oh!*" Ben stared as the flames sparkled and crackled and burnt red and green and silver.

CRACK! A log of the apple wood split into two halves, and a small green child no bigger than Ben's hand stepped out of the fire and on to the floor beside him.

"Good evening," said the child.

Ben couldn't speak. He stared and stared at the little green figure, and looked into the fire, and then back again.

"If you're wondering where I come from," said the child, "I come from the apple log. I'm an apple child – how do you do, and what's your name?"

"I'm Ben," said Ben, still staring.

The apple child smiled. "Glad to meet you. And now, how about supper?"

Ben shook his head. "I'm sorry," he said, "I've nothing but a few old seed potatoes in a sack in the yard."

"Let's fetch them in," said the apple child. "There's nothing like a big baked potato."

Ben shook his head again. How could an apple child know that seed potatoes were poor shrivelled green things that could never be eaten? He went slowly out into the bitterly cold wind.

The sack was behind the door, just where the farmer had left it. The sack was there – but it wasn't nearly empty. To Ben's amazement, it was full to splitting with fine, clean, rich yellow potatoes. He chose four of the biggest and hurried back inside.

"Put them to bake on the fire," said the apple child. "I'm hungry!"

Ben slept well that night. He woke in the morning to find the sun bursting in through the window.

"Good morning," said a cheerful voice. "Shall we have eggs for our breakfast?"

Ben rubbed his eyes, and saw the apple child standing beside him holding two big brown eggs.

"That's a splendid black hen you have," said the apple child. "She's hiding a nest behind the blackberry bushes."

"But she's been gone for months," Ben said. "I was certain the fox had had her for dinner."

"Not she," said the apple child. "And I found a few good nuts on the walnut tree."

Ben looked curiously at the apple child. Had he grown in the night? It seemed to Ben that he had, although he was still the smallest child he had ever seen. And what magic was he working? Even Ben's bare cold room felt full of warmth and the smell of apple wood and sunshine and flowers.

"Well?" asked the apple child. "Have you decided? Soft or hard-boiled eggs?"

Ben and the apple child settled down happily. It seemed to Ben that the cottage was always warm now, and full of sunlight. The black hen was laying steadily, and his two little brown and white bantams had reappeared, clucking happily, from under the hawthorn hedge. Ben was quite sure

79

that he had, with his very own eyes, seen them both being carried off by foxes, but he smiled and collected the small brown eggs. When Mrs Wutherlop from next door came by to ask if he could spare an egg or two he was more than willing, and he took the crusty bread she offered him in exchange with pleasure.

Strong green shoots sprang up in Ben's bare back garden, and he found that he was growing the finest cabbages and leeks and carrots in the village – more than enough for him and the apple child. Ben filled his wheelbarrow and took his extra vegetables to the shop, and came home chinking real money in his pocket, the first he had had for weeks and months and years. He didn't see old Mrs Crabbitty in the opposite cottage peering out of her misted and cobwebbed windows as he hopped along the road, and he didn't see Mrs Crabbitty poking and sniffing at the crisp green cabbages and creamy white leeks in the shop, her little black eyes gleaming greedily.

"Them's Ben's leeks, you says? And carrotses? Well, well, well..." and she shuffled home, mumbling to herself.

That evening Mrs Crabbitty came knocking on Ben's door.

"Seems things is a-picking up for you, young man," she said, her eyes slipping and sliding as she stared over Ben's shoulder into the glowing room beyond. "Seems as if you found yourself a liddle slip of luck."

Ben felt uncomfortable. He had never liked Mrs Crabbitty, with her peeking nose and her small black shiny eyes, but he knew she lived on what she could beg or borrow from the village, and had nothing of her own.

"Would you care to come in?" he asked, with a small sigh.

"There now," said Mrs Crabbitty, whisking through the door and settling herself by the crackling flames. "There's a fine fire."

Ben looked around. He had last seen the apple child toasting his toes on the hearth, but there was no sign of him now. He felt Mrs Crabbitty's beady black eyes searching round and about, and he hastily turned back to her.

"Looking for something?" Mrs Crabbitty asked him. "Or, maybe, for someone?"

Ben shook his head.

Mrs Crabbitty brought two shining steel knitting needles out of her pocket, and a small ball of grey, greasy wool. She began to knit, and while she knitted she swayed a little and hummed a strange tuneless drone.

Ben couldn't take his eyes away from the flashing silver needles, and when Mrs Crabbitty began to ask him questions about the garden, and the little black hen, and the never-ending supply of wood in the basket, he was unable to stop himself telling her all about his visit to the moonlit orchard, and the coming of the apple child.

"So, you just threw the wood on the fire, young man?" Mrs Crabbitty asked, clicking her needles and swaying.

"Yes," Ben said, his voice creeping away from him like a small sly snake.

"Then what's good for the young will be good for us old ones," said Mrs Crabbitty. She sat up straight, and snapped the shining needles together. Hauling herself up on to her feet she nodded at Ben.

"I'll be off to my own poor place," she said. "But

I'll be having a special sort of a blaze tonight, nows I knows what's what."

Ben watched her scuttle away. He was surprised to see that she didn't go straight home, but went away down the road, pulling her shawl round her shoulders.

Mrs Crabbitty scurried along towards the end of the village street.

"I'll fetch meself a slice of luck," she said, rubbing her hands together. A sharp gust of wind caught at her shawl and tossed it away in front of her until it caught on the branch of a tall tree standing at the very edge of the orchard.

"Dratted wind!" Mrs Crabbitty struggled towards the tree, and pulled at her shawl. It came with a wrench, and brought a shower of twigs and a twisted branch with it that fell at her feet.

"Well, well, well." Mrs Crabbitty bent and picked up the branch. "Maybe here's me luck, after all." And she hurried back towards her dark and dusty house. The wind grew louder than ever, and rushed in between the apple trees with a shriek so that they shook and quivered under the moon.

Mrs Crabbitty's fire was a mere glimmer in the darkness of her dusty, spidered room, but she fed it with pieces of loose bark until an uncertain flame flickered. Then she took the entire branch, and pushed it into the back of the fireplace. First one green flame and then another sprang up, but there was no heat to be felt; the blaze was as cold as the fire at the heart of a bitter green emerald.

"Now, I'd like company, so's all me work gets done for me. No reason why lazy boys should have all the luck."

Mrs Crabbitty peered into the grate, and the branch began to twist. There was a splitting and a splintering, and something shapeless came slithering out on to the hearth. It squirmed itself into a long-bodied, bandy-legged, large-headed creature, and then it began to grow. Mrs Crabbitty, watching open-mouthed, saw it bulge and stretch and twist until it was pressed up against her cracked and yellowed ceiling. Only then did it stop growing. Mrs Crabbitty reached behind her for her chair, and sat down with a flump. The creature turned and looked at her with its glassy eyes, and she stared back.

84

"What kind of a thing ezactly are you?"

"Elder bogle," growled the creature in a voice that was full of gravel and grit.

"Ah," said Mrs Crabbitty. "And why ain't you an apple child to help a poor woman?"

"Elder branch." The bogle pointed a bent and wrinkled finger at the smouldering fire.

"Is that so? And what ezactly can you do?"

A movement on the table caught Mrs Crabbitty's eye, and turning she saw a bowl of small apples blackening and rotting as she watched. The elder bogle watched as well, and as the last apple shrank into nothingness he smiled a sour and twisted smile.

Mrs Crabbitty sucked her lower lip thoughtfully.

"If you and I is to live together," she said, "I'll thank you to leave *my* goodies alone."

The elder bogle gave her a cold look, but it said nothing. It folded itself up into a dark heap, and appeared to go to sleep. Mrs Crabbitty took her shawl and climbed up to bed. Before she went to sleep she thought for a long time and then, smiling, closed her eyes.

Ben and the apple child heard about the elder

bogle from Mrs Wutherlop. She came knocking on the cottage door the next morning, carrying a jug of sour milk and a dish of moulded and pitted plums.

"What is it?" Ben asked. "What's happened?"

Mrs Wutherlop began to cry. "Mrs Crabbitty," she sobbed, "her said that if I don't give her milk each day she'd witch me. And I says no, an' she whistles up a horrible bogle thing, an' now there's nothing fit to eat in my larder, nor yet a green leaf in my garden, an' the kitten's crying its heart out. And it's the same for all the folks in the village who won't do what she says, up comes that there bogle, an' the milk turns sour an' the hens don't lay an' the pigsies are as thin as a rail. And us doesn't know what to do!" Mrs Wutherlop sat down on Ben's step and threw her apron over her head.

Ben patted Mrs Wutherlop's shoulder, but she went on crying. He hurried out to his own garden, but there everything was growing and green. He peeped over the fence, and saw at once the terrible bareness where Mrs Wutherlop's carrots and onions and potatoes had been. Even the holly tree was as bare as a winter's oak.

86

Ben picked up a basket and filled it with walnuts and eggs and apples and cabbages from his larder, and put it down beside the still sobbing Mrs Wutherlop. Then he went to see if the apple child knew what might be happening.

The apple child was, as usual, sitting and feeding the fire with twigs and sticks.

"There's something terrible come to the village!" Ben said. The apple child nodded. "Mrs Crabbitty's slice of luck."

Ben squatted down by the child. "Is there anything we can do?" he asked. "Poor Mrs Wutherlop's crying and crying and crying. Can you make her garden grow again like you made mine?"

The apple child stood up and stretched. "There's not room for an elder bogle and an apple child in the one village," he said.

"What do you mean?" Ben asked anxiously. "You don't mean you're going to go away?"

"We'll see," said the apple child. "Elder bogles are strong, but they're not always clever."

"I'll come with you," said Ben, as the apple child moved towards the door. "I'm not scared – well, not very."

*　　*　　*

Ben and the apple child walked out of the cottage and past Mrs Wutherlop. She had stopped crying, and was holding the basket of vegetables closely to herself as if they were protection. When she saw Ben and the apple child going across to Mrs Crabbitty's cottage she followed them.

Mrs Crabbitty was sitting on a bench at the side of her cracked and crumbling cottage. She was shelling a bowl of fresh peas, and six or seven fine fat hens were clucking and fussing about her feet. Piled up against her cottage wall were strings of onions, jugs of thick golden cream, sweet cured hams, pies and pastries with shining sugar crusts, russet apples and a huge grass twist of straw-berries. There was no sign of the elder bogle.

Mrs Crabbitty looked up and saw Ben and the apple child. Her face looked pinched and sour, as if she too was growing moulded and rotten.

"And what would you be after?" Her voice sounded thinner and sharper. "These things is mine, mind you. Mrs Crabbitty's found her luck."

Ben didn't know what to say. The apple child

was saying nothing at all. He was looking up at the little windows of the cottage where a dark shadow was moving behind the dust and the cobwebs. There was a slithering and a sliding, and the doorway was filled with the twisted shape of the elder bogle. When it saw the apple child it began to hiss, and its eyes glowed greedily.

"Now, my pet," said Mrs Crabbitty, "what's troubling you?"

The elder bogle cracked its bony knuckles and stretched out its skinny arm towards the apple child.

"Go away," it growled. It waved at the house behind it, and the village in front. "MINE! ALL MINE!"

The apple child still said nothing, but he shook his head. The elder bogle began to snarl.

"Fight!" Its teeth were long and yellow, and Ben took a step backwards. He was glad to find Mrs Wutherlop close behind him, and she put a large freckled hand on his shoulder.

"FIGHT!" The elder bogle was circling round the apple child, growling and sniffing and snarling.

"Wait." The child's voice was small but very clear. "I won't fight, but I challenge you: a test – a test of strength."

89

The elder bogle and Mrs Crabbitty both laughed a sour, cackling laugh, and then the elder bogle nodded its heavy head. It turned round and round until it saw the tall old pine tree that sheltered Mrs Crabbitty's cottage. Crouching down, it clasped its long arms about the tree's huge trunk, and then with a grunt and a heave it wrenched the quivering tree out of the ground. With a gravelly snarl it stood up, the pine on its shoulder, and began to make its way up the mountain towards a wind-blasted tree at the very top.

Mrs Crabbitty gave a shrill scream of laughter. "There, my fine friends. He can carry the tallest tree on his shoulder, all the way up to the top and all the way down. A test of strength, you says – I says the same – can you do as well? Look, see, already he's at the top!"

Ben watched in horror. Even with the massive pine tree on his back the elder bogle was leaping and jumping across the rough mountainside. The apple child was as light as the wind, how could he possibly carry any such load?

The apple child seemed unconcerned. He was choosing an apple from Mrs Wutherlop's basket, and when he had carefully chosen one he polished it.

"Huzzah! Huzzah! Here comes my pet, my pretty poppet!" Mrs Crabbitty waved her bony arms in the air as the elder bogle came loping back down the village street. It was still carrying the pine tree on one shoulder, and on the other shoulder was a massive branch from the stricken tree on the top of the mountain. With a snarl of victory it slid to a stop in front of Mrs Crabbitty, and tossed the huge pine tree right over her cottage. Ben felt the ground shudder under his feet, and a trembling in the air as the old pine crashed to the earth.

"YOU!" shouted the elder bogle, sneering down at the apple child.

The apple child nodded. He touched Ben with his hand, and sprang away up the street towards the mountain. He ran as if he was dancing, and the apple trees fluttered and rustled as he passed them. He ran as if he was flying, and the birds swooped lower and circled above his head. He spun three times round the tree at the very top of the mountain, and then ran back to the village with the ease of a stream flowing over a grassy bank. He touched Ben once again, and the time that he had taken was less than half that taken by the elder bogle.

"I say the apple child wins!" called out Ben, but his voice was uncertain. The elder bogle and Mrs Crabbitty snorted, and the elder bogle stamped its leathery foot so hard that a grey dust flew up, making Ben cough and rub his eyes.

"You called for a test of strength," said Mrs Crabbitty, shaking her fist. "And I says as my pretty pet is the winner!"

The elder bogle grinned a wicked yellow-toothed grin, and rubbed its gnarled and withered hands together. Mrs Crabbitty pointed at Ben. "You and yours have had your chances. So, be off with you!"

Ben's shoulders drooped.

"We'll go," he said, and turned away.

"Just one moment."

The apple child was standing in front of them. In his hand was an apple, and as they all stared at him he broke it in half, and showed it to the elder bogle.

"Six pips," he said. "Six seeds – SO! You carried

one tree, but I carried *six* apple trees up and round the mountain … six tiny living trees in one apple. I am the winner, and I claim the village for my own."

The elder bogle let out a shriek that made Ben clutch his ears. Mrs Crabbitty screamed a high piercing scream.

"Tricksied! We've been tricksied!"

The elder bogle howled and wailed and stamped its foot. The earth beneath Ben's feet shook, and a swirl of grey-green dust flew up into the air. The elder bogle stamped again, and the ground split beneath it.

"No! My poppitty! My pet!" Mrs Crabbitty sank on to her knees, but the elder bogle was already gone. All that was left was a clump of green leaves.

"Oh! Oh! Oh!" said Mrs Crabbitty, and she turned and scuttled into her cottage like a small frightened spider.

The apple child looked after her. "She'll do no harm now," he said.

Mrs Wutherlop took Ben's arm.

"A nice cup of tea wouldn't come amiss. Eh, what a carry on!"

Ben turned to the apple child. "Is it all over? Should we go home?"

"Yes," said the apple child. "Hurry on home."

Something in his voice made Ben stare at him. "Aren't you coming too?"

The apple child shook his head. "I'll be about," he said. "Here and there..."

Ben sighed. "I shall miss you," he said.

Mrs Wutherlop patted Ben's shoulder. "You can come and sit with me for company," she said. "And I've a kitten that's looking for a home."

The apple child waved, and moved towards the apple trees on the mountainside.

They were heavy with ripe red apples, and the sheep grazing beneath were fat and thickly fleeced. Even the bare mountainside was flushed with patches of soft green grass and clusters of bushes.

"Goodbye, Ben," said the apple child.

"Goodbye," said Ben, "and thank you." He could feel tears at the back of his eyes, and there was a lump in his throat. Turning, he ran after the warm and comfortable figure of Mrs Wutherlop. The apple child paused for a moment, and then slipped in among the apple trees.

On the edge of the deepening blue sky a golden harvest moon was rising, and high above a single star watched over the village. Shadows stretched out from the richly laden trees, like thick ribbons of warm black velvet binding the small houses and cottages safely together, and the moon smiled as it sailed on over the mountain.

The Boy Who
Walked on Water

Once there was a boy who could walk on
water. He lived with his grandfather and his mother
on an island where the sea crept into the land with
long twisting fingers, and rivers and streams
wound round and round and in and out until the
island was a patchwork of rocks and hills and
fields sewn together with the shining strips of
ditches and dykes.

Although the island was small it was not easy to
travel from East to West, or North to South, for
there were always saltwater lakes to walk around
or rivers or streams to cross. The boy, Fergal, had
no such problem. As soon as he could walk at all

he walked as easily on water as he did on the ground. He walked on the streams and the lakes and the rivers, and even the sea. "Look at that," said his mother. "Now, there's a gift." His grandfather said nothing. He was a fisherman, as were all the islanders, and he had seen and thought many things while he was rocking in his boat on the northern seas. A grandson who could walk on water was certainly strange, but there was, most likely, a reason for it somewhere.

When Fergal was a little boy he did not notice that he was different from other children. After all, every winter, when cold winds came sweeping down from the North, the sea froze, and the lakes and rivers and streams of the island turned into solid blocks of clouded silver ice. All the children whooped and slithered and slid, and Fergal slid with them. Even when the spring came and the ice melted away, Fergal played happily with his friends. Some of them were good at running races. Others were expert at walking on wooden stilts. Ailsa could swing herself round and round in cartwheels. Fergal could walk on water. If the older children looked at him strangely and whispered behind their hands, Fergal never noticed. The adults said nothing at all. They agreed with Fergal's grandfather. There was probably a reason somewhere, and if there wasn't, well, it did the boy no harm, nor anyone else as far as they could see.

As Fergal grew, things changed, and not for the better. He was a shy, quiet boy who wanted nothing more than to be like everyone else – but no one else could do what he did. Two or three children began to tease him, and soon, the others joined in.

"Fergal's a water beetle!" they called after him.

Their parents told them to leave Fergal alone. "He can't help the way he is," they said. "Don't bother him." But the children took no notice. They ran after Fergal and danced in circles round him.

"Fergal the frog!" "Maybe he's been bewitched!" "He's not like us!" "Fergal's STRANGE!"

Ailsa slipped her hand into his, and told him not to mind.

Fergal became quieter still, and more thoughtful. His mother noticed that he now hopped across the stream on the stepping-stones, and walked all the way down to the bridge to cross the river. When it was warm enough to splash and swim in the sea, Fergal was nowhere to be seen.

"Where have you been?" Ailsa asked him.

"I had to help my mother in the house," Fergal told her, but his mother was sitting down on the harbour's edge mending nets.

As time went by the children slowly forgot that Fergal had once been able to walk on water. All they remembered was that he was in some way different, and however hard he tried he was never at the centre of the laughing groups of boys and girls. Only Ailsa called for him to join them as they ran races on the sand or jumped from rock to rock. Only Ailsa caught his hand and dragged him into games of tag or catch-me-as-you-can. If Ailsa was busy looking after her little brothers and sisters Fergal was left alone. He would go for long solitary walks North and South and East and West, but he never once walked on water.

"Be careful," his grandfather warned him. "Gifts are given to be used, not to be hidden."

Fergal turned away.

*　　*　　*

The storm came early one morning as the last fishing boat sailed into the harbour. It was the most terrible storm that the islanders had ever lived through; far more wild than the storm that had drowned Fergal's father on the day that Fergal was born. Black clouds came swirling up and covered the island in darkness, and tearing winds wrenched bushes out of the earth and hurled them into the air. For three days and nights the sea roared and growled and clawed at the island until the shores and cliffs were raw and ragged. The fishermen's boats were snatched from the harbour and tossed into the howling tempest as if they were walnut shells, and the huge rocks and slabs of granite that made up the harbour wall were cracked and splintered until they lurched, broken, into the heaving waves around them.

When at last the storm was over the islanders walked silently down to the shore. They did not speak. There was nothing to say. There was no harbour, no protecting wall and not one boat. The younger children ran about picking up strips of seaweed and scraps of sailcloth that lay scattered on the sand and stones, but the older ones looked anxiously at their parents.

"Will we build the harbour again?" a boy asked his father.

His father shook his head. "What for?" he said, and his voice was bleak. "We have no boats to keep there."

"We can find wood and make more boats," said a girl.

Her mother sighed. "You know there are no trees here. We trade our fish for wood ... and without our boats there will be no fish."

"No fish, and nothing else besides," said an old man. "All our livelihood is gone. There's nothing left for us now."

"Look! Look!"

Ailsa's father had climbed out on the cliff above the tumbled heaps of stone where the harbour wall had stood. Now he was shouting and waving his arms. "A boat!" he shouted. "I can see a boat!" Other islanders rushed to join him, and Ailsa and Fergal scrambled after them. They shaded their eyes and stared over the sea, and wondered about the dark speck way out across the heaving and rolling waves.

"Whatever it is we must fetch it in!" said Ailsa's father. "If it's nothing but wreckage we can save the wood ... and if it is a boat we can begin again! We can search for our fishing boats ... we can fish ... we can live!" And he tore off his heavy boots and coat and leapt down the cliff to plunge into the cold water.

"No! No!" Ailsa ran after her father, but she was too late. He was already striding deeper and deeper into the swell of the tide. An incoming wave knocked him off balance and Ailsa gasped as he sank beneath the steel-grey water, but he came up spluttering. He was still looking ahead to the horizon. The islanders watched silently as he began to swim with short jerky strokes. None of them were strong or able swimmers. They believed, like most fishermen, that it was better to drown quickly than to swim on and on and die a slow and lingering death.

Ailsa's face was white. Even as her father stared steadily ahead of him, so she watched her father.

His black head, glistening like a seal, moved further and further away from the shore and safety.

Fergal looked at Ailsa, and then out across the rippling sea. Was it a boat? If it was, it was tossing and teasing at the edge of sight. Surely no one could swim so far. Fergal turned, and walked to the water's edge. As he stepped out from the sand there was a roar from the rocks above. "Murdo's in trouble! He's sinking! He can't go any further!"

No one saw Fergal take his first step. They were far too intent on shouting and calling to Ailsa's father to see that Fergal, for the first time in his life, was paddling – that he was not walking on water but splashing in the shallow lapping waves. Fergal stood still. His gift was gone.

"Fergal! FERGAL!" It was Ailsa, flying down the shore towards him. "Fergal – save him! Save my father!"

"Go, boy, go!" His grandfather was beside him. "Now's the time, Murdo's drowning! Help him, boy, help him! Walk on water!"

Fergal took another step, and the waves splashed against him so that he stumbled. He turned, his face as white as Ailsa's, and held out his hands.

104

"Ailsa!" he said. "It won't work for me any more!"

Ailsa stared at him, her eyes wide.

"You do it," said Fergal, and he touched her arm. "Walk on water, Ailsa – GO!"

And Ailsa was walking on the water. She was walking, she was running, she was skimming the surface like a seagull.

The islanders held their breath as she flew over the tossing waves, over the white foam. She reached her father as he struggled to the surface for the third time, coughing and gasping, his lungs bursting with the desire for air. Ailsa reached down to him, and there were the two of them standing hand in hand on the water as if it were nothing more than a shifting sheet of glass under their feet. Together they turned to the horizon.

All the men and women and children standing on the cliff top rubbed their eyes, and wondered if they had really seen what they thought they had seen. They shook their heads and told each other that the mist was coming up over the sea, and it was easy to see strange things in mist. They told the children not to be so foolish. How could they

105

imagine that two people could walk together on water, hand in hand? But all the same, Ailsa and her father were gone. Had they both drowned? Or would they come back? *Could* they come back?

"We'll watch and wait," said Fergal's grandfather, and it was agreed that this was all that could be done.

It was almost dark when Ailsa and her father came back to the island. The sun was sinking low into the West, and stars were creeping up the violet sky. The little boat came dancing over the waves with the evening wind behind it, its sail bellying out triumphantly. The islanders raised a cheer that shook the seabirds off the rocks, and hurried to haul the boat high up on the shingle. Ailsa and her father were carried shoulder high, up and away to where a fire was blazing on the headland to light them home. There was singing and dancing and feasting, and when Ailsa's father told how he and Ailsa had seen more of their boats beached on a bare island not too far to the North the cheering reached the moon itself.

"Murdo has saved us all!" a boy shouted.

"Aye! Aye! Three cheers for Murdo and Ailsa!"

"Murdo, who swam to save us!"

"Murdo, the seal swimmer!"

Ailsa's father nodded his head, but Ailsa jumped up.

"We didn't swim!" she said. "It was Fergal. Fergal gave me his gift! We walked on water!"

The islanders nodded and smiled at Ailsa, but they went on singing and celebrating. Soon it was understood that Murdo the seal swimmer had swum halfway across the ocean to save the island. And Ailsa? Some said Ailsa had swum after him ... and a few said she walked on water. Most islanders shook their heads. Hadn't they told the same story of Fergal ... and was that true? No!

Ailsa slipped away from the flickering lights of the fire. "Fergal!" she called into the darkness, "Fergal!"

There was no answer. Ailsa went down to the shore. Fergal was sitting on a stone, his feet in the water, listening to the waves as they whispered and sighed in and out of the little stones under his toes.

"Fergal!" said Ailsa, and she ran to him. "Fergal, I've lost your gift! When Father and I found the boat it left us. Will it come back to you?"

Fergal shook his head. "I don't think so," he said, and he looked down. "I don't want it. I've never known what water felt like before today. It feels like cold silk. It's so beautiful!"

Ailsa shivered. "Beautiful," she said, "but dangerous too."

Fergal picked up a pebble and tossed it into the water. It fell with a splash, and Ailsa laughed and threw another pebble after it. Then she caught at Fergal's hand, and pulled him to his feet. "Come on," she said. "I can hear the fiddler playing up on the cliff. Come and dance!"

"We can dance here," said Fergal, and he and Ailsa held hands and twirled and whirled round and round on the sandy shore. Neither of them noticed the pebbles as they bobbed back up to the surface of the sea as easily as if they were corks, and floated slowly away upon the outgoing tide.

The Old Potmender
and the Tin Tea Kettle

Not so very long ago there was a potmender who lived with his wife in a tiny cottage tucked away on the side of a hill. Every day he walked down to the village below and went from house to house looking for work. The people of the village were not rich, and if their saucepans and frying pans and baking tins wore out they had no money to buy new ones. They waited for the potmender to call, and he would put a metal patch over the hole and solder it into place. Then they could use the pan again because it wouldn't leak any more – or if it did, it was only a little. They paid the potmender a few pennies for his help and he would

111

walk home happily, jingling his money in his pocket.

The days and the weeks and the years went by and the potmender grew old. There didn't seem to be so many pots and pans to mend, and those that did need mending belonged to the poorest villagers who had hardly a penny to spare. As well as growing old the potmender grew hungry, and his wife grew angry. One evening he came home with nothing at all. He came slowly up the path to his house, opened the door and put down his bag of tools as quietly as he could. Looking nervously around he tiptoed inside, hung up his coat and crept towards his tattered old armchair.

"Potmender! Is that you at last?" His wife came screeching towards him, her hair on end and a wooden spoon in her hand. Behind her the tin tea kettle bubbled and hissed on the fire.

"Yes, dear," said the potmender, and he sighed.

"And how much money have you made today?"

The potmender sighed again. "Nothing."

"And why not?" His wife banged the spoon on the table and the potmender jumped. "I suppose you've been mending pots and pans for free."

112

The potmender sighed for the third time. "They didn't have any money," he said. "But they did thank me very much."

"Did they indeed?" said his wife. "And since when did a thank you ever pay for bread and cheese?"

The potmender fished in his pocket. "Old Granny Green gave me two silver buttons."

"Buttons!" His wife leapt in the air in fury. "Buttons! How are we to eat? How are we to mend the roof? How are we going to pay the rent? Buttons, indeed!" And each time she said "Buttons!" she banged the table, and each time she came closer and closer to the potmender until she was waving the spoon right in front of his nose. The tin tea kettle hopped and fizzed on the fire and rattled its lid, but the potmender's wife took no notice. She glared at the potmender.

"You go straight out of that door," she said, "and don't come back until you've got a pocketful of money! Not buttons, mind – *money!*"

"Oh, wife," the potmender said wearily, "I'll try and do better tomorrow... I'm so tired now. Couldn't I just sit by the fire and have a little bread and cheese? And maybe a pickle or two, to help it down?"

"*No!*" shouted his wife, and she waved the spoon more wildly than ever. "There'll be no bread and cheese until you bring in some money! Not a crumb! Not a rind! Not the sniff of a pickle! *Be off with you!*"

The potmender went slowly to the door.

"I'm going," he said. "I'm going." He pulled his coat down and began to struggle into it, muttering as he did so. "I do wish she'd leave me alone. I try my best. I really do. I wish she'd go away somewhere, so I could have a little peace. But where could she go? Nowhere that's far enough away to give me a rest..." He shook his head as he picked up his bag of tools. "Nowhere ... maybe even that's too near. I wish she'd go away to ... to the other side of Nowhere!" He put out his hand to open the door, and then stopped.

It was quiet. Amazingly quiet. The old potmender rubbed his eyes and looked round.

"Wife?" he said. "Wife? Where are you?"

There was no answer.

"*Wife!*" The potmender hunted round the bare little room. He opened an empty cupboard and peered under the table.

"*Wife*! Where are you? Please come back!"

There was no sound except for the bubbling of the kettle. The potmender sat down and gazed into the fire. "Wherever can she be? One minute she was here, and the next – gone! It's very odd, it is indeed."

"No it's not. *Sssssssss*!"

The potmender sat bolt upright. Whoever had spoken had a hissing, spitting voice. "Who's that?" he asked nervously. "And where are you?"

There was an even louder hiss. "*Sssssssss*! Here I am!" And the tin tea kettle swung itself off the fire and winked at the potmender. "Aren't you going to thank me?"

The potmender couldn't say anything. He sat and stared. The tin tea kettle began to hiss and bubble and dance up and down.

"No more shouting! No more nagging! You can sit in front of the fire and toast your toes in peace and quiet … for ever and ever and ever!"

The potmender went on staring. "I don't understand," he said. "What's happened? Where's my wife?"

"How stupid you are!" the tin tea kettle hissed.

"You wished your wife would go away, didn't you? And so she has – I made your wish come true! She's blown away – blown away to the other side of Nowhere! Oh, how clever, how clever, how clever I am!" And the tea kettle spun itself round in a circle and puffed steam all over the room.

"Oh!" said the potmender, and he jumped up. "Oh, my poor wife! What have I done? Where is she? Oh, dearie, dearie me!" He hurried to the door. "I didn't mean it – whatever will she be thinking? Poor thing – she'll be so lonely all by herself on the other side of wherever it is – I must find her!" He opened the door and looked back at the tea kettle. "Please tell me where to go – where should I start?"

The tin tea kettle let out a long and piercing whistle of disgust. "*Sssssssssssssss*! So *this* is all the thanks I get! But you'll never find her. Never, never, never! Tee hee hee! You wanted her on the other side of Nowhere, and that's where she is ... for ever and ever and ever!" And it blew one last hiss of steam and disappeared up the chimney with a hop and a skip.

The old potmender swung his toolbag onto his

shoulder and shut the door behind him. He shivered as the wind sliced through his thin coat.

"If that tea kettle won't help me I'll go on my own," he said to himself. "The other side of Nowhere! Wherever can that be? I know, I'll go down to the village. Someone there is sure to be able to tell me. *Brrrr!* Perhaps I'll feel warmer if I walk a little faster." And he set off down the path as the first few drops of rain began to fall.

The night grew darker and darker, and the rain grew heavier. The old potmender began to slip and slide as he hurried along, and he wished that he had brought a lantern. Branches tugged at his coat, and twisted roots caught at his feet.

"The path to the village is never as hard as this," the potmender muttered to himself as he struggled through a tangle of thorns. "I must have lost my way—" And as he spoke a gust of wind and rain rushed at him from behind and sent him rolling over and over into the darkness.

The potmender sat up and rubbed his head. It was so dark he could see nothing at all, but he was out of the wind and rain. Something heavy was lying on his feet; he put out a hand and found his tool-bag. Carefully he felt all around. He seemed to be lying on something soft ... leaves, he thought, and he yawned. "At least it's warm and dry in here," he said. "I might as well stay put until morning." He yawned again. "I'm so tired..." He pulled his tool-bag under his head as a knobbly pillow, shut his eyes and went to sleep.

The old potmender woke up slowly. He was aching all over, and his head was sore. He opened his eyes, trying to remember where he was, and saw the sun shining in from a wide opening between tall grey rocks.

"I must have fallen into a cave," he said, and began to struggle to his feet. He was halfway up when he stopped, and sniffed. He could smell a wonderful warm sweet smell. He sniffed again. "Hot chocolate!" said the potmender, and he scrambled out of the cave.

Outside the sun was bright and the sky was blue.

"I'm sure I've never been here before," said the potmender, as he looked at the hillside of grass and stones. "Wherever can I be? And – goodness gracious me! *Whatever* is that down there?"

Down below him a river ran splashing and gurgling between the rocks. A dark brown river; a river that steamed and bubbled and boiled … and smelt of cosy evenings by the fire with comforting mugs of hot cocoa.

The potmender scratched his head. "I do believe it's a hot-chocolate river! It really is! It's very strange, very strange indeed. Maybe I'm going the right way to find my wife after all … when you think about it, the other side of Nowhere is sure to be different from our village." And the potmender nodded to himself and began climbing down towards the chocolate river, his bag of tools jangling on his back.

Halfway down he paused. Something was running along the riverbank. Or was it running? The potmender screwed up his eyes. No, it wasn't running. It was hopping; hopping on one leg and waving its arms like a windmill.

"Oh dear," said the potmender. "I do hope it's not dangerous." He hesitated for a moment. "It isn't very big. And it might be able to tell me if I'm on the right road." He went on climbing over the rocks and stones.

By the time the potmender reached the river the smell of hot sweet chocolate was very strong indeed. It made his eyes water and his stomach rumble with hunger, but he was too busy gazing at the odd little figure in front of him to think about eating or drinking. It had stopped hopping and was crouched on a rock that leant right over the steaming river. The potmender edged a little closer.

"Why," he said to himself, "it's fishing up hot chocolate in a tiddly old saucepan! Maybe it'd let me have a sip or two?" He took a step nearer. As he did so the little creature pulled the saucepan out of the river and boiling chocolate splashed all over its small furry feet.

"*Oh! Oh! Oh!*" it shrieked, and began hopping and jumping just as it had done before. The potmender shrank back as it whirled its saucepan round and round. Gradually it began to calm down, but it went on whimpering and moaning. The pot-mender saw that its feet were covered in blisters and boils.

Poor little thing, he thought, and then he caught sight of the saucepan. *"Goodness!"* He was so surprised he spoke out loud. "That's the biggest hole I've ever seen!"

"What? What's that?" The creature pricked up its long ears. "What did you say?"

The potmender took the saucepan. "Just look at that hole!" he said. "You can't use it like that!"

"But I must! I'm the Drinker!"

The potmender shook his head. "You'll not be doing much drinking out of a pan like that."

"No," said the Drinker, and its ears drooped. "I don't."

"I could mend this," the potmender said, and he turned the little pan over and over. "It's not worn through everywhere." He swung his bag off his shoulder and sat down. The Drinker squatted down beside him and looked hopefully at the tools the potmender was laying out on the grass.

"Can you really make it better?" it asked.

"I should think so," the potmender said. "I'll need a few sticks to make a fire, though."

The Drinker jumped up. "Easy!" It skipped off, and was back in no time carrying an armful of

121

sticks and twigs and dry leaves.

"Grand!" The potmender built a small fire and lit it with his tinderbox. The Drinker sat as close as it could and watched.

"What will you do?" it asked.

"Why, mend this hole, of course," said the pot-mender. "Then your pan will be as good as new."

The Drinker looked at the saucepan in surprise. "I thought it *was* new. I thought it was meant to be like that."

The potmender blew on his fire. The flames began to crackle and to burn, and he pulled out a piece of metal from his bag. "Here," he said. "I'll put this over the hole and solder it in place, and – oh!"

"What is it?" The Drinker stared at him.

"How could I have forgotten? I used my last little end of solder on Granny Green's frying-pan."

The Drinker began to tremble. "Is that bad? Is it very bad?"

The potmender sighed, and pushed his hands into his pockets. "There's nothing I can do without a scrap of solder," he said sadly.

"Oooh," moaned the Drinker. "Oooooh."

"Wait!" The potmender shook his coat and

something jingled. "Look here! The two silver buttons Granny gave me! I can use one of those..." And he set to work.

By the time the potmender had finished the sun was high in the sky. He wiped his forehead and handed the little saucepan to the Drinker.

"Try it now," he said.

The Drinker smiled an enormous smile and scurried to the river's edge. Carefully it bent down, and carefully it filled the pan.

"It's *full!*" it called out. "It hasn't spilled a drop! Oh, now I can drink and drink and drink!" And it lifted the panful of steaming chocolate and drank it in one gulp.

"That would burn my mouth for sure," the pot-mender said as he tidied up his tools.

The Drinker swung round. "Thank you!"

The potmender sighed, and picked up his bag. "I'd best be on my way," he said. "I shouldn't really have stopped so long. I'm looking for my wife. I don't suppose you'd know where the other side of Nowhere is?"

The Drinker put down its saucepan. "Try the

other side of the river."

The potmender was so surprised that he dropped his bag.

"Oh yes," said the Drinker. "Over there on the other side of the river is Somewhere, and in Somewhere you'll find the Somebodies. They know about *everything*, so they're sure to be able to tell you where Nowhere is. And then – pip! – you just have to find the other side of it." The Drinker leant down and filled its saucepan again. "Have a little drink before you go."

"Thank you kindly." The potmender took the saucepan gratefully and blew on the chocolate to cool it. As he sipped he looked up and down the bubbling river. "That's splendid news, that is. The Somebodies, you say? Just splendid. Where's the bridge?"

"Bridge? There's no bridge."

The potmender choked on his last mouthful. "But how will I get across?"

There was a silence. The Drinker opened and shut his mouth several times, and pulled at his whiskers. "I don't know," it said at last.

"Is there a boat?" The potmender looked anxious.

"I must get across to the other side and find those Somebody folk. My wife's sure to be wondering why I'm not there to fetch her home."

"No boat." The Drinker drooped.

The potmender sat down and held his head. "Oh, dearie, dearie, dearie."

"*Eeeek!*" The Drinker leapt into the air. "I know! I know! The Freezer! He'll *freeze* the river, and then you can slide across on the chocolate ice!"

The potmender looked up at the wildly spinning Drinker.

"What's that?"

"The Freezer! Quick! Call him now!"

"And he'll get me across the river?"

"Yes! Yes! He'll freeze it!" The Drinker sprang at the potmender and pulled him to his feet. "Now! Call his name! As loudly as you can!"

The potmender cupped his hands round his mouth. "Mr Freezer!"

"*Louder!*" said the Drinker. "*Louder!*" And he hopped a little way up the hill.

The potmender tried again. "*Mr Freezer! Mr Freezer!*"

"*Louder!*" The Drinker was moving further and further away. "Louder! Louder..." And his own

125

voice faded.

The potmender took a deep breath. "MR FREEZER! MR FREEZER! Oh, please come! PLEASE COME, MR FREEZER!"

A chilly breeze sprang up. A grey cloud swept across the sun and was swiftly followed by others, each darker than the one before. A flurry of snowflakes swirled round the old potmender's head, and an icy wind cut through his thin coat and made him shiver. The snow hissed and spat as it drove down the hill and into the river, and clouds of steam billowed up into the darkening sky. The potmender shuddered and pulled his coat tightly round him.

"WHO ARE YOU THAT DARES TO CALL ME FROM MY HOME AMONG THE SNOWS AND STORMS?"

The potmender turned slowly, his teeth chattering. An enormous figure was staring down at him with glittering frosty eyes.

"Excuse me, my Lord," the potmender said, his voice shaking, "but I need to cross the river..."

"AND WHAT CONCERN IS THAT OF MINE?"

The potmender shook his head. "None, sir. I see

that now, and I'm ever so sorry to have bothered you. I just thought..."

"Thought? What did you think?"

"That you could ... that you could freeze the river. Well, that is, if it's not too much trouble..."

The Freezer swung round, the pale folds of his cloak whirling about him. The potmender sank to his knees, his arms over his head.

"BUT IT IS A TROUBLE! WHAT WILL YOU GIVE ME FOR MY TROUBLE?"

"I have very little," the potmender whispered. "All I have are my tools. You can have my tools... Or a silver button..."

"WHAT USE ARE THOSE TO ME?" The Freezer flicked his long blue fingers, and a hailstorm burst into the frozen air. The potmender crouched lower as the hailstones rattled about him.

"I HAVE NO NEED OF SUCH THINGS. NO ... YOU MUST GIVE ME YOUR COAT!" And the Freezer laughed.

The Freezer's laugh chilled the potmender as he had never been chilled before. He nodded, unable to speak, and slowly, for his hands were numb with cold, pulled off his skinny old coat.

"MY THANKS, POTMENDER!" The Freezer tossed the

coat onto his back, and the potmender saw that the Freezer's cloak was made entirely of scarves and coats and cloaks and jackets and shawls, all of them worn to threads and heaped one upon another. "AND NOW – BE GONE!"

There was such a stinging slap of snow on the potmender's face that he shut his eyes. He felt himself sliding, and could not stop. He was so cold that he could not think. Where was he? What was he doing? As snowflakes and hailstones drove against him he fought his way onwards, staggering at each step. He came to a heap of rocks and began slowly to crawl over them. The wind shrieked and wailed, and needles of icy sleet beat down on him. The old potmender sank to the ground. The cold crept up and over him, and he slipped into a frozen sleep.

Above the potmender the winds raged and howled a while longer. Then there was a whistle, a clear cold whistle from the frozen North. Swirling round in a circle, the winds raced away, and the clouds drifted apart. The sun came out and warmed the earth and the snow began to melt.

"Potmender! Potmender!"

The potmender rubbed his eyes and sat up. Had he really heard something? It was the faintest of cries, and far, far away.

"Potmender! Potmender!" It was fainter still, a thin thread of sound.

"*Wife!*" The potmender struggled to his feet. "Where are you? I'm coming!" And he began to hurry along the path as fast as he could go. He puffed as he scrambled round boulders and through long tangled grass, and it was only when he stopped to catch his breath that he noticed the snow had gone.

The potmender stared in amazement. "There's no sign of all that snow! And it's quite warm!" He climbed up a small bank and looked around. "Well, I never! There's the hot-chocolate river – and it's behind me! I must have crossed it in all that snow, and I never knew." He sat down and wiped his forehead. "So here I am on the other side. Why, this must be Somewhere! I must hurry along and find those Somebodies ... whoever they might be." And he set off along the winding track in front of him.

*   *   *

Gradually the track became a path, and the path became a road. It was a fine road, an important-looking road, and it made the potmender feel that he shouldn't really be walking along it. The road was so wide and clean, and he was so dusty and dirty. Every so often the road gave a little twitch and a sniff; when the potmender took to trotting along in the ditch it gave a loud sigh of relief.

I wonder where I should look for these Somebodies, the potmender thought. I expect they live somewhere really grand. A road like this must be going somewhere very wonderful. He pulled his belt a little tighter and sighed. "I just hope they have something there for me to eat."

"Good morning, dear sir!"

"Why, dear sir, good morning to you!"

The potmender looked up from his ditch. A hugely round person was rolling slowly down the road. Another hugely round person was rolling in the other direction, and they met with a gentle bump. They took no notice of the potmender.

"A fine day!"

"A very fine day!"

"A very, very, very fine day!" And they bowed and nodded and smiled at each other.

"Excuse me!" The potmender scrambled out of his ditch. The road shuddered, but the two hugely round people went on bobbing and beaming exactly as if he had never spoken.

"Excuse me," the potmender said again, "but would you please very kindly tell me if you are the Somebodies?"

The first round person quivered. "Did you hear something, dear sir?"

"Why, dear sir, I think that I did."

"Should we answer, dear sir?"

The second round person gave the potmender the speediest of glances.

"No, dear sir. I think we need not." And it smiled a fat wide smile and bowed and nodded and bowed again.

The potmender shook his head. Then he pinched himself and rattled his bag of tools. "It seems to me that I'm as real now as ever I was," he said to himself, "so how come they don't seem to see me?" He took a step forward and cleared his throat.

"Ahem. Excuse me, but I'm looking for the Somebodies. Is it you, or isn't it?"

The road gave a horrified wriggle, but the two hugely round people merely raised their eyebrows at each other.

"Did it speak again, dear sir?"

"You know, dear sir, I think that it did."

"Did it address us by name, dear sir?"

"Dear sir, dear sir, I fear that it didn't." The second hugely round person rolled even closer to the first, and whispered in a loud and carrying whisper, "It would seem, dear sir, *that it doesn't know who we are!*" And both of them flapped their hands in horror and rolled their eyes.

"Such ignorance, dear sir!"

"Indeed, dear sir. Should we tell him?"

"It would, dear sir, be only kind."

And the two hugely round people rolled themselves in a circle so that they were facing the pot-mender. They bowed to each other once more, and then spoke.

"Know, you small and dusty thing—"

"that *we*, you unimportant nothing—"

"are indeed..." they paused and bowed deeply, "...THE SOMEBODIES!"

The potmender stared. The two Somebodies were beaming their fat wide smiles at each other, and patting each other warmly on the back.

"Well said, dear sir!"

"Dear sir, well said!"

"Just a moment!" The potmender went on staring. "Just a moment! You say *you* are the Somebodies?"

The two Somebodies chuckled fatly.

"We are indeed!"

"Indeed we are!"

The potmender put down his bag of tools. All sorts of thoughts were tumbling through his head.

"Somebodies?" he said at last. "You call yourselves *Somebodies?* When you couldn't even be bothered to give me a good morning or a how d'you do? Let me tell you, that's not being a Somebody. Where I come from a Somebody is someone who is kind, and helpful, and who has time for you. Somebody who'll ask you if you're lost, and show you the way. Somebody who'll help you find your poor lost wife who's somewhere in the middle of the other side of Nowhere and likely to stay there for

ever and ever if all folk round here are like you. You're not Somebodies, you two. You're not anything at all! You're just puffed up with your own importance. You're – you're *Nobodies*!"

WHOOOOOOOOOOOOOOOOOOOOOSH!

The rush of air knocked the potmender head over heels, and the road trembled underneath him. He rolled over and over into his friendly ditch, and as he climbed out again his eyes widened. The Somebodies were shrivelling and shrinking, and as they shrank they squeaked and squawked and finally burst into tears.

"*Whooooooooooooooooooooo*!" they sobbed. "*Whoooooo-ooooo! Oooooooo! Oooooooooo…*"

The potmender stared. The Somebodies looked like nothing so much as two crumpled heaps of clothes sitting on the edge of the road.

"*Oooooh*! Whatever shall we do?" they whimpered. "We're not Somebodies any more. We're nothing. Why, we must be – we must be – *Nobodies*!" And they began to wail louder than ever.

The potmender took a step towards them, not quite sure what to do. They looked so different he could hardly believe they had been the pompous and self-important Somebodies only a moment before.

"There, there," he said. "It's not that bad, being a Nobody. I'm a Nobody, and my wife's a Nobody, and we get on very well with it."

The Nobodies crept towards him.

"We're so sorry we were rude," whispered one.

"Dear sir, do forgive us!" whispered the other.

The potmender shrugged. "Don't you worry," he said. "We all make mistakes... But just don't do it again, that's all. And now if you'd be kind enough to tell me where I can find the other side of Nowhere, I'd be most grateful. I must be off to find my wife."

Instead of answering, the two Nobodies began to sob loudly. "Nowhere!" they cried, "Nowhere! Oh, if we're Nobodies now we can't be living in Somewhere any more. Oh dear, oh dear, oh dear, we must be living in Nowhere!"

"Is that right?" The potmender picked up his bag and began to smile. "You mean I'm in Nowhere already? That *is* good news. Can you tell me where the other side is?"

There was no answer. The two Nobodies were sniffing, snuffling and blowing their noses.

"If we're Nobodies," one of them said slowly, "can we do *nothing*?"

The other one gave an excited little squeak. "Oh yes! Nothing to do!"

"Nothing all day!"

"Nothing every day!"

And they began patting each other on the back and bowing and bobbing and smiling.

The potmender sighed and left them to it.

"At least I'm doing well so far," he said, as he trudged away. "I'm sure to come to the other side sooner or later." He took a deep breath. "Wife! *Wife!* I DON'T KNOW IF YOU CAN HEAR ME BUT I'M ON MY WAY!"

"Tee hee hee! *Sssssssssssssssss*! Tee hee hee! That's what *you* think!"

The potmender stopped dead. There, hissing and hopping on the path in front of him, was the tin tea kettle.

"Oh no!" said the potmender. "Not you again!" He frowned fiercely. "I'm on my way. I'll soon have

136

my wife back, whatever you may think."

"Tee hee hee!" The tea kettle spun round and round and steam puffed out behind him. "It's a joke, it's a joke, don't you see what a joke it is? Tee hee hee!"

The potmender gripped his bag of tools tightly and went on walking. He was sure he was on the right road, and a tin tea kettle wasn't going to stop him now.

"*Sssssssssssssssss*!" The tea kettle danced in front of him blowing smoke rings. "You're so *stupid*! Don't you see? Your wife blew away to the other side of Nowhere … and the other side of Nowhere is Somewhere. You found yourself in Somewhere and what did you do? You turned it into Nowhere … you're going in circles, in circles, in circles!" And the tin tea kettle began to bubble and to boil madly as it cackled and snorted with glee.

The potmender stood quite still. He could hardly believe what the tin tea kettle was saying. He had come so far, and now it seemed he had only been walking in circles.

"You mean, you mean I was in the right place where I was before?" he asked. "Oh, my poor wife.

Oh, what a bother this all is..." And he sat down wearily on the edge of the road.

"Tee hee! What a joke what a joke what a ... *sssssssssss*..." The tin tea kettle staggered. "*Sssssssssss*..." it hissed, and it was no longer laughing. "*Ssssss* ... help! Help!" It sank down at the potmender's feet. "Help me, potmender," it fizzled. "I think ... I've ... burst my sides ... help me..." And a thin trickle of water spread slowly into the ground.

The potmender folded his arms. "That serves you right," he said. "It really does. You're a nasty, wicked tea kettle and I don't see why I should help you after all you've done."

The tea kettle dribbled a little more. "If ... you don't help me ..." it hissed, "you'll ... never see your ... wife ... again."

The potmender stroked his chin thoughtfully. It certainly looked as if the tea kettle couldn't move. He came a little closer, and walked round it, keeping a safe distance in case this was another of its tricks.

"Hmm," he said, "you've split your side. There's quite a gap there."

"If ... you ... mend me ... I'll ... make ... sure ... you ... and your wife ... are together ... for ever..."

138

"That's all very well," said the potmender. "But how do I know you're not playing another of your silly tricks?"

The tin tea kettle moaned. "I'll ... show ... you."

The potmender watched suspiciously as the kettle began to rock itself to and fro. It murmured and it muttered in its thin weak voice and the faintest sizzling came from deep inside it. A tiny puff of steam floated into the air, and inside a small picture grew. Dimly the potmender could see his wife floating round and round in a never-ending circle of mist and smoke. She was calling out and, even though he couldn't hear her, the potmender knew she was calling for him.

"I'm coming to find you, wife!" he shouted, but the picture faded away.

"Right!" The potmender began hurrying to and fro collecting dry sticks. He made up his fire, and opened his bag.

"Help!" whimpered the tin tea kettle. "Mend ... me..."

"And what do you think I'm doing?" the potmender asked. He blew on the sticks and the flames burned high. He hunted in his bag for a piece of mending metal and felt for the silver button in his pocket.

"Dearie me," he said, and he sighed. "Fancy wasting a fine silver button on a wicked old tin tea kettle."

"*Sssssssssssssss*," said the tea kettle weakly. "*Sssssssssssss*…"

The potmender began to heat his soldering iron. "Here we go. Although if it weren't for wanting my wife back I'd never be mending you at all." And he set to work patching up the tea kettle's side.

As the potmender finished, he blew out the fire. "There," he said. "You're not as good as new, but you'll do."

The tin tea kettle got up slowly. "*Sssssssssss*," it whispered. "*Sssssssss*!"

The potmender buckled up his bag of tools. "And now you'll send me and my wife home, if you please."

"*Ssssssssssssssssss*!" hissed the tea kettle, and it began to spin. "Tee hee! Tee hee!" And as it spun it began to bubble and boil. "Here we go! *Sssssssss*! Here we go!" The potmender found himself spinning behind the kettle, faster and faster and faster.

"Hey!" he shouted, "What's going on? Where's my wife?"

"Here she *isssssssssssss*!" the tea kettle fizzled and spat. "Here she *issssss*!" And as the potmender spun he saw his wife spinning beside him, round and round and round.

"Wife!" he called. "Wife!" He held out his hand, but she was spinning much too fast to catch it.

"*Sssssssssssssssssss*! Tee heeeee! Here you are! Together again! Together for ever! What a joke!" And the potmender saw the tea kettle hop and skip out of the circle that was spinning him and his wife up and down and round and round. The kettle slid away, and as it went the potmender could see puffs of steam shooting up into the air around it. Its lid was rattling with laughter, and it danced and sizzled with excitement.

"Together for ever! Spinning for ever! Round and round and—"

BAANNNNNGGGGGGGGG!

The explosion was so loud that the potmender clutched his ears as he fell in a heap on the ground. At the other side of the circle his wife screamed. Little pieces of tin flew into the air all around them, and clouds of steam gushed up. For a moment the potmender could see nothing at all, and then a figure came walking towards him through the steam.

"*Wife!*"

"Oh, potmender! Is it really you at last?"

And the potmender and his wife held hands and smiled and smiled.

"Well, well, well," said the potmender. "Whoever would have believed such goings on! But now it's time to be getting back home ... whichever way that might be!"

His wife glanced around. "I do believe we're on the path below our cottage!" She looked a little sideways at the potmender, and she blushed. "Potmender, dear," she said, "how would you like some supper? You must be ever so tired and hungry after such a terrible time as you've had." She let go of the potmender's hand, and twisted her apron. "I was thinking, up there in that circle. I was thinking, maybe I've been a little hard on you of late."

"Were you, wife?" asked the potmender, and he took her hand again as they walked towards their cottage.

"Yes," said his wife. "You do your best. I know that ... and I have been shouting a little too much. Just now and then."

The potmender opened his mouth in surprise, and then closed it firmly. "It's been a hard time for both of us, wife," was all he said.

"So we'll go home, shall we?" said his wife. "There's some bread and cheese in the cupboard."

"That would be fine," said the potmender. "And maybe a pickle or two?"

"And a pickle or two," his wife agreed.

And as they walked into their tiny cottage the potmender thought he could hear the merest whisper of a hiss and a chuckle...

Singing to the Sun

Once there was a lord who did not believe in love, and he married a lady who only believed in gold. At the end of a year a son was born, and the lord stooped down to the cradle to look.

"One day," he said, "this child will be the most powerful lord in all the land. Every man, woman and child will tremble as he passes, and even the mightiest of my horses will bow his head as this boy walks by."

"I will not bow," said the small tabby cat who sat by the hearth, but nobody heard her except the court jester ... and no one ever took any account of what he saw or heard or thought.

"No, no!" said the haughty lady. "He will be the wealthiest lord in all the land. Why, even the rats that run in his kitchens will eat from dishes of purest gold."

"Hmm," said the tabby cat. "And what use is gold when you are hungry and thirsty and far away from the places of men?"

"Exactly so, little one," said the jester, and he shook his head so that the bells on his hat jingled and rang. The baby smiled and held out his arms, but his mother frowned and carried him away.

The years rolled by. The mighty lord grew older and greyer, but he did not grow wiser. He sent armies this way and that to crush and defeat the kings who lived nearby, and sometimes he won, but more often he was defeated. His lands grew smaller and poorer, and this did not please his wife at all. She grew meaner and meaner, until she counted every bite of meat and every sip of water. She kept the one golden coin that was left in a silver chest, and she kept the silver chest in a leaden coffer. The leaden coffer she kept in a wooden box, and she wore all three keys on a chain round her neck.

In the upstairs nurseries the baby grew older and taller until he grew into a little boy, and then he moved to the rooms of state and grew taller still until he became a young man. He had been christened Thorfinn, but few people knew him by his name. His father always forgot, and his mother never remembered. Sometimes Thorfinn went downstairs to the kitchens to talk to the jester (who was now very thin) and the tabby cat (who was now very fat), but most of the time he was kept poring over ancient books. The books his father gave him spoke of the best way to win battles, and the books his mother gave him were full of charms and spells that showed the best way to turn pebbles into gold.

On Thorfinn's eighteenth birthday there were no presents, but his mother and father met together to talk about his future.

"It will soon be time for our son to marry," said the mighty lord. "He must marry the daughter of the most powerful king in all the world, and then he will be lord of all the kingdom. His lands will stretch North and South and East and West ...

further by far than an eagle can fly."

"No, no!" said the haughty lady. "He must marry the daughter of the wealthiest king in all the world, and then he will be lord of all the gold and the silver and the diamonds and the rubies in the kingdom. His buttons will be sapphires, his shoes will shine with emeralds, and even his shadow will be the finest black silk velvet."

The tabby cat was sitting on the windowsill.

"And what would Thorfinn like for *himself*?" she asked, but there was no one to listen to her. Thorfinn was sitting in the ancient library studying the royal rules of battling with dragons, and the jester was walking on the hills and listening to the winds.

It was the jester who brought the news. No one was ever quite sure where he had heard it, but then nobody ever asked the jester how he knew what he knew. He came to the mighty lord and the haughty lady as they sat over their breakfast.

"My lord," he said, "my lady. The King of the Golden Mountains has three daughters who wish to be married. The king is tired and old, and he has divided his kingdom between them. One daughter will be given all his lands, and power over everything that grows and lives there. One daughter will be given all his wealth, together with the gold mines, the silver mines, the diamond mines and the lakes of pearls. The third daughter—"

"STOP!" shouted the lord, and the lady sprang to her feet and clapped her hands.

"We have no need to hear any more! Quick – quick – saddle the horses! Call for our son! He must leave at once!"

Thorfinn was sent for, and he came slowly into the room, looking anxious. He was not used to speaking to anyone other than the jester and the tabby cat.

"Son," said his father, "you are to ride at once to the Golden Mountains. You will go to the king, and you will tell him that you will marry the princess who brings land and power."

"No, no, NO!" The lady shook her head so hard that her necklace broke and the beads scattered all over the floor.

"Son! Listen to me! You are to ride at once to the

Golden Mountains. You will go to the king, and you will tell him that you will marry the princess who brings wealth – the gold mines, the silver mines, the diamond mines and the lakes of pearls."

"No, NO, NO!" The lord banged his fist on the table so hard that the wood splintered beneath his hand. "You must marry land and power!"

"NO, NO, NO!" The lady stamped her foot so hard that the stone floor cracked in three places. "Wealth! You must marry wealth!"

Thorfinn said nothing as his father and mother shouted louder and louder and louder. He sat down on the window seat and stroked the tabby cat.

The tabby cat looked at the jester, who was patiently waiting by the door.

"I would like to know about the third princess," she said, so softly that only the jester could hear her.

The jester smiled. "The third princess brings nothing and everything," he said. "She brings happiness, and love."

"Ah," said the tabby cat. "That is everything."

The lord and the lady argued until the sun was high in the sky, and they were too worn out and angry to speak another word.

The jester stepped towards them and bowed low.

"My lord," he said, "my lady. The King of the Golden Mountains will, without a doubt, welcome your son with open arms. But there are others who will be less welcome, and so he has set a task for all those who come hoping for power, or riches, or even merely happiness."

The lord and the lady sat up.

"What task?" croaked the lord.

"What kind of task?" whispered the lady.

The jester bowed again. "When Lord Thorfinn comes to the palace he will be taken to the king's great hall. There he will see the three princesses sitting on three thrones. All three are beautiful, but one is pearl pale, with hair as fair as a field of ripened corn at sunrise. One princess is rose pink, with hair as red as a chestnut just cracked open from the shell. One princess is ebony dark, with hair as black as the depths of a midnight river."

"Enough! Enough!" shouted the lord. "Which is

the princess with the lands and the power?"

"No, no, NO!" snapped the lady. "Which is the princess with the gold?"

The jester shook his head. "Nobody knows. No one, that is, except the King of the Golden Mountains. And that is the task. Lord Thorfinn – and the other princes and lords and young men and old men who come to try their luck – will have to guess. They are to have one chance, and one chance only, and if they guess wrong –" the jester shrugged – "why, there are hungry wolves on the Golden Mountains."

The mighty lord and the haughty lady looked at each other. The jester looked at Thorfinn. Thorfinn stopped stroking the tabby cat, and the tabby cat meeowed and rubbed her head against his hand as he stood up.

"I will go to the Golden Mountains," Thorfinn said. "I have read and read until my mind is sore, and I would like to go out into the world."

The lord and the lady heaved a huge sigh of relief. Even they with their hard and shrivelled hearts were unwilling to order their son to risk being torn apart by hungry wolves. If, however, Thorfinn himself chose to go out and seek his fortune – well, that was a *very* different matter. His father called for horses, and his mother called for a jerkin of silver and a cloak of golden velvet.

"And a sword encrusted with emeralds to buckle at our son's side," she said.

"And six of my finest soldiers to ride in front and behind," said the lord. "Jester – see that it is done."

The jester spread out his empty hands.

"My lord," he said, "and my lady. There are no horses left in the stables, and the last of the soldiers marched away after last year's war. There is no jerkin of silver, nor cloak of golden velvet, and there is no gold left to buy such things. Neither is there a sword encrusted with emeralds ... but the young lord is welcome to ride my donkey, and I have a cloak of wool to keep him warm."

"Will you come with me?" Thorfinn asked. "We can ride the donkey turn and turn about." He bent down and picked up the tabby cat and tucked her under his arm. "And you can come too, my friend."

And that was the way it was. The mighty lord and

the haughty lady were not pleased when they saw their son ride off to seek his fortune on a donkey with only a jester and a tabby cat for company, but there was nothing that they could do or say to change the way things were. All they could do was to make Thorfinn promise over and over again that he would do his best to choose power or wealth ... and even as his shadow faded from the pathway his mother was still calling, "Gold! Gold! Gold..."

The road to the Golden Mountains was long and hard, but Thorfinn was happy. He stared around him in wonder as the donkey clip-clopped along, and the jester told him stories of the towns and villages and farms that they passed.

"How much you know!" Thorfinn said. "I know nothing at all ... except that wars cost more than peace, and it is very very hard to turn pebbles into gold."

The jester laughed, but the tabby cat nodded.

"Both those things are good to know," she said. "It is also good to know that one has much to learn."

At last the road led up to the gates of the King of the Golden Mountains. Beyond the gates was a crowd of lords and princes, young men and old, all hoping to win the hand of one of the princesses. Thorfinn and the jester took their place in the line, and the tabby cat walked beside them.

Little by little Thorfinn and the jester moved nearer and nearer to the palace. From far away came the sounds of cries and moaning, but when Thorfinn asked the jester if he knew what the reason could be the jester shook his head.

"The wolves will be fat tonight," said the tabby cat, but she spoke so quietly that Thorfinn could not hear her.

When Thorfinn and the jester were led into the king's great hall Thorfinn's eyes grew wide. The three princesses were sitting on three tall thrones, and all three were more beautiful than Thorfinn could ever have imagined. The pearl pale princess was dressed in tissue of silver, and her corn gold hair rippled down to the floor. The rose pink princess was dressed in silks the colour of an ocean wave, and her glowing chestnut hair shimmered in the light. The princess who was ebony dark wore ruby red velvet, and her midnight black hair curled and twirled and danced around her head. Not one of them smiled when Thorfinn stood in front of them; they stayed as still and as silent as statues.

"Ahem," said the king. "It is time for you to make your choice, young man. You may look as long as you wish – but you may not speak a word to my daughters, and they will not speak a word to you. When you are ready, come to me – and tell me which daughter brings power, which wealth, and which love. If you choose correctly my daughters will curtsey to you, and then you must choose which one you will take as your bride."

The King of the Golden Mountains swept away to his own throne at the other end of the hall, and musicians began to play soft music as Thorfinn stared and stared at the princesses.

"How can I choose?" he asked the jester. "I know nothing about princesses, and I have no way of telling which is which. How can I choose?"

The jester touched his arm. "Ask their father the

king if you are permitted to take one hair from each of their heads."

Thorfinn looked up in surprise. "A hair?" he said.

"Yes," said the jester, and Thorfinn did as he was told ... although his hand trembled as he took a hair from each princess in turn.

"That was well done," the jester said. He walked across to the musicians, and bowed to a man playing the violin. The man stopped playing, and the jester bowed again.

"May I?" he asked, and as the man nodded the jester took his bow and threaded it with the silver blonde hair. "Now, play!" he said.

The musician took the bow and began to play, and as he played the other musicians fell silent. The tune was harsh and strong, and Thorfinn could hear the sound of bugles blowing and heavy armoured feet marching ... marching ... marching.

"Enough," said the jester, and he took the bow and pulled away the silver blonde hair. "Now ..." and he threaded the bow with the chestnut hair, and it shone between his fingers. "Play!"

This time all Thorfinn could hear was the clink clink clink of coins tumbling and falling, and the murmur of dulled voices counting ... counting ... counting.

"That will do," said the jester. He snapped off the chestnut hair, and gently, carefully threaded the bow with gleaming black. "Play," he said. "Play."

As the first few notes sang out Thorfinn put out a hand to steady himself against the wall. He could hear the sweetest birdsong, and children laughing. He could hear women singing lullabies to their babies, and old men humming as they sat and dozed in the sun. He could hear young men and women whispering secrets to each other, and in and out danced a little tune that was so happy Thorfinn thought his heart would break in two.

"Now," said the jester, "tell the king what you know."

Thorfinn went to the king. "The pearl pale princess brings power," he said. "And the rose pink princess brings gold. And the princess as dark as midnight brings happiness and love."

"You are right," said the king, and the three princesses stood up, and swept Thorfinn three deep curtsies.

"Choose," said the king. "Choose from Power, Wealth and Love. Choose your bride, and my good wishes go with you."

Thorfinn looked at the Princess of Power, and he thought of his father endlessly fighting wars so that he might seize a little land here, a little land there ... or, more often, lose it. He looked at the Princess of Wealth, and he thought of his mother endlessly scrimping and saving and valuing nothing if it was not made of gold. Then he looked at the third princess, and he thought of the endlessly long lonely years he had spent growing up in his old cold castle.

"I have lived with power and wealth," he said, "and power and wealth are hard as stone. I have never lived with love, and I do not know what it is like ... but I think I would like to be happy. I choose the princess who is as dark as midnight."

The king bowed, and the Princess of Love swept another deep curtsey.

"Thank you, my lord," she said, and she smiled a smile that made Thorfinn hold out his arms to her. "Thank you, but I do not choose you." She turned to the jester. "You are the wise one, and you are the man I will marry." And she took the jester by the hand, and the jester threw off his cap of bells and the two of them ran out of the king's palace and off and away to live happily ever after.

"Oh," said Thorfinn, and he bent down and picked up the jester's cap.

"Will you not take power, or wealth?" asked the king.

Thorfinn shook his head. "No," he said. "I shall travel the world until I am as wise as the jester..." and he walked slowly out of the palace and up the road. Behind him walked the tabby cat, and as she went she looked up at the sun and she sang.

For Maria